SMOKE SCREEN

**CALUMET
EDITIONS**

Minneapolis

First Edition May 2024
Smoke Screen © 2024 by Carol Rincker.
All rights reserved.

10 9 8 7 6 5 4 3 2 1
ISBN: 978-1-962834-12-4
Cover and book design by Gary Lindberg

SMOKE SCREEN

CAROL RINCKER

CALUMET EDITIONS

Minneapolis

Water reflects not only clouds and trees and cliffs,
but all the infinite variations of mind and spirit we bring to it.
—Sigurd Olson

Olsen-Chubbuck Bison Kill Site Near Kit Carson, Colorado

A thick blanket of fog crept through the valley, its fingers silently grasping the nearby cliffs. Before long, a series of good-natured currents transformed into an all-out squall. As the wind changed, a sudden blast nearly whipped Sage from her feet. She imagined being snatched from the rocky bluff to the valley below. Maybe the childhood urge to balance on a large boulder had been fun. Now, it seemed downright suicidal. The thought of plummeting a couple hundred feet kicked in her common sense. She stepped back from the ledge by several long paces.

The lightweight poncho slapped her legs, and as she moved farther toward safe ground, a blast of driving rain began. Her phone pulsed somewhere in her jacket under the wind-whipped poncho. She chose to ignore it, fearing she might falter on the slippery rocks or wet undergrowth. A flash of thought reminded her of stampeding bison driven over the edge by ancient hunters. Her hand rummaged under the poncho. At last, she felt the cold phone.

Sage stared at the incoming call. Crystal. At least for a moment her friend's voice was clear. Maybe the transmission wasn't so bad after all. Or else the spirits were suddenly on her side. She shouted to be heard over another cold blast of wind.

"Hey, how'd you track me here?"

"That's what phones do, remember? Last I recall, Colorado was still part of the planet."

"Right. But talk fast." Sage kept her back to the wind. "My poncho is getting stiff, and my teeth are starting to rattle." She reached to pull the hood forward, but the wind tried to whip it from her head. There was a frustrated sigh from Crystal.

"Hey, y'all. Pay attention, will you? I've got lots to fill you in on before your damn wind gets any worse."

"You sound weird. Is everything okay?" After a lengthy pause, Sage began to suspect a bad connection after all. Or something worse. It was odd her friend would call now when she was due home in less than a week. She waited. "Hurry it up. My toes are getting numb."

Crystal's Southern twang was oddly flat, and there was a hint of reserve. "Lots going on back here."

"Okay, go on."

"I take it Judd hasn't called you? No one's seen your father since last Tuesday. He took MT into Two Harbors for their shared grocery run."

"And your point?" The cold was unbearable, and Sage was sure her fingers would freeze.

"MT ended up with his coffee beans, so she went to return them yesterday. Looked like his studio had been trashed. So like I said, Colin's nowhere to be found. And then there's more interesting news. I went to pick up mail yesterday, and there was background chatter at the post office. Word has it that jerk Holton Denys is planting some comments about going after your property."

"That's ridiculous. It's not for sale—and won't be. At least not in my lifetime."

"Your father hasn't toyed with the idea?"

"Of course not. It would never cross his mind." Sage hoped the chit-chat would end. The cold wind made her shake, and her teeth had begun to chatter. She felt like a marble statue but colder. "Huh. Weird—I mean about the studio and my dad. As for the fire, I've been tracking it on my weather app. Looks like it's been pretty dry. And there's no sign of rain, right?"

"Nope. No rain headed this way. At least not yet. But it's windy. Way windy. I'm hearing talk about evacuation—the powers that be are thinking ahead for once."

"Cripe. Just what we need. Okay. With luck, I'll hustle out tomorrow—early."

"I'm guessing you might have to pack up your dad's studio if he doesn't show up soon." Anyway, sharpen up those psychic powers of yours. Looks like y'all are gonna need 'em. As for me, life is calmer in Alabama, even when a hurricane hits Mobile Bay. I'm fix'n to close up for now and hit the road for home. Besides, I know my mother will breathe easier."

"Crys? Wait—what?" The connection was gone. Getting a head start for home made sense, and she had a good excuse. Given the forecast, outdoor work would certainly be delayed. She felt lucky not to be a student again—this time around, she wouldn't be forced to battle the whims of Mother Nature. She scrambled from the boulder and signaled to Rick, her graduate assistant.

"Despite my love of Colorado, I have to leave—sooner than I thought. Think you can handle this bunch?"

She made a quick grab for her cap as the wind tried to flip it toward the valley. She imagined again what it might look like as hunters drove massive herds of bison over the cliff's edge. She'd always viewed it as a strange and foreboding place. Today, it was even more so—almost menacing, with the icy grayness and raging wind. Still letting her thoughts wander, she imagined ancient spirits swirling around her. She doubted sun would help. Climbing into her aging Volkswagen bus, she wondered what kind of storm awaited in Minnesota.

Windward Trail
North of Lake Superior
St. Louis County, Minnesota

As a child, Colin's studio held wonders that mesmerized Sage. On some days, she watched clumsy blocks of clay become bowls and platters, mugs and jars to meet the desires of his well-heeled admirers. On other days, when Colin needed inspiration or wanted to charm his daughters, art would rise from his infinite imagination. Life-sized ceramic ravens might perch on ceiling beams. Cherubs dangled by fishing line near windows, waiting to take off on fantastical journeys. Today, it seemed his presence was nearby, yet she felt no sense of peace or comfort.

In a far corner, a massive worktable held an array of bowls and wide platters awaiting their first firing. On a series of shelves, perfectly aligned vases reminded Sage of a miniature terracotta army ready to report for glazing and a last trip to the kiln. A huge, covered jar with her father's typical raku handiwork posed on a wooden pedestal.

At one end of the room, a large area surrounded a two-sided fireplace. Folding chairs leaned nearby for gatherings. A large window overlooked a nearby path to the house. Books, papers and assorted tools were scattered in a rough heap on the floor. She guessed the visitor— or visitors—hadn't completed their task, whatever that had been. For Sage, it was a stroke of luck in the midst of chaos. Still, an odd sense of foreboding settled over the studio. With an ability to detect woodland danger as a child, Sage had brought her talent to adult life. This time, the feeling cut straight to her throat, and the quiver through her neck came with a faint but detectable sputter of fatherly presence.

"Damn. I can sense your aura, and you're as overbearing as ever." She felt a sudden wave of queasiness. Was it the hollow feeling of her father's studio that left her so unsettled? Or maybe the scent of smoke that carried an unnerving message of caution? The occasional sharp smell of a burning forest was stronger than she'd expected. How would she know if—or when—it was time to bail?

Sage fought to steady herself. Damn her tendency for vertigo. It was like looking down at the bison kill. The studio walls shifted, then oozed into angular corners. The morning breeze murmured through the open windows, stirring a smoky vortex of haze against the sunlight. Some unreachable part of him was there, but the familiar sound of her mother's old wind chimes was gone. They usually hung near her father's desk, but today, that space was empty. Odd.

She tried to put her thought fragments in sensible order. Endless conjectures hovered in her head, yet she couldn't shake them. "This feeling you're sending me, Colin, am I supposed to guess it means you're dead? Or just off on one of your fatherly junkets and too far away to reach? I could use your help here, you know. You've always encouraged my bohemian side."

His car was parked near the garage, yet he lived for canoe trips, whether near or far. With all the nearby lakes, he could have struck off on a portage. He truly could be anywhere. The thought of reporting his disappearance terrified her. Who knew how long he'd already been away? Thank God she'd returned home.

Sage murmured quietly to her father as if he were present. "I guess you heard about that developer who's been eyeing our property. You always warned me to watch for guys like that. I saw him in town a couple days ago." She took a long breath. "I was ready to jump in the van and be gone. Thank God he didn't follow me. Anyway, intuition told me he's trying to find an angle. It's like he's quietly breathing down my neck to assess our property. So far, he's minding his own business, keeping in the background. That means, for now, it's all innuendo."

Sage recalled her father's warnings about childhood strangers. This case seemed to fit, even though he appeared on the outside to be a savvy adult.

"There's no way our place is going to be part of his magic kingdom. And these days, I think he might have trouble finding a local resort developer who'd be willing to tolerate him. Anyway, Colin, thanks for listening. Sure wish I knew where you are."

Sage cradled her coffee and bent over her father's desk. On her left, she quickly scanned a pile of memos. Next, she leaned to the other side and wrote in the dust, "I'm here, Colin. Love you. Where are you?" It would be clear that she'd written the note because she often addressed her father by his first name.

The scent of hot sun on pine drifted past the studio, even though now and then it was partly masked by smokiness from burning wood and vegetation. It was a deceptive odor, one that brought campfires and marshmallows to mind. Lazy summer nights with the songs of frogs, nighthawks and the occasional chorus of coyotes. But now, grasping that glorious smell as a harbinger of danger was hard to fathom. Somewhere in the midst of downed pines and hardwoods, dried by summers of sun and wind, a spark had been the beginning of what looked to be a potential inferno. In response, resort owners hosed their cabins, volunteers dug trenches, and low-flying planes sent showers of red fire retardant over square miles of forest. A devastating summer wind one year had left acre upon acre of blowdowns, setting the stage for a hellhole of fire nearly two decades later. Had the cause been a lightning strike? There had been plenty of storms lately, though little rain. Or maybe a careless camper? She hated to imagine that the reason was more sinister.

Dropping into Colin's chair, Sage tipped back and propped her boots on her father's desk, not caring if they ground into the film of dried clay and dust. Shards of a large platter were scattered like puzzle pieces. The largest lay near the center of the room, while smaller pieces skittered outward. Had whoever moved it tripped? Worse yet, maybe they'd deliberately moved to a more open area and slammed it to the floor. Hard to tell, but what looked like a sign of hate and hostility was alarming.

7

A large wall map of the Superior National Forest was speckled with colored pins. Red stood for portages on favorite routes and blue for those that were merely so-so. Nearby, other assorted maps and charts covered the walls. A lone purple pin represented a father-and-daughter game they'd used to play. Sage stood and pulled it from the map, then cradled it in her palm. Only two blues stood out in the spread of red. She moved her finger along the forest border, tracing its ragged southern edge, then scanned north along the Boundary Waters Canoe Area Wilderness—a gem of more than a million acres—and north to the jagged border of Canada. Acres and acres of backcountry. Endless miles of primal streams, jutting rocks, and perhaps even next year's national Christmas tree. There was an endless maze of where he could be. Knowing her father's hiking and paddling habits, he wouldn't have gone far. At least not without a grand plan for one of his major expeditions—and she'd have known about that. But still, why the mess? Had someone been scared off?

* * *

"Geez, I didn't expect you until Thursday." Judd, Colin's apprentice, stormed through the door. "Make more noise next time."

"You're the one who came charging in. I got Rick, my grad student, to take over my class, and that put me on the road a couple days early. I'd have lost my mind back there, not knowing anything. At least being here takes some edge off the panic," Sage took a long breath and ran a hand over her face and through her hair. "Anyway, most of the excavating's done, and they're looking at core samples now. I don't need to be on hand for that. Rick's got my number, so we're set." She watched Judd closely. He seemed more tightly wound than usual.

"Did you tell them that's about as close to doing real archaeology as they'll ever get? They'll probably all end up as office workers." Judd scowled down his nose, waiting for her response.

Not that old theme again. She decided to shift gears. "What is it they say?" she mused. "Oh, right. Something like 'discovered missing.' As far as my father is concerned, what the hell kind of doublespeak is that? If he took off somewhere, he had a reason."

"I think it partly means no one knows exactly when he took off." As Judd edged away, he waited for her reaction. "We're not sure when he disappeared. Or, in our case, if." He seemed jumpy, and perhaps he sensed she'd vehemently disagree. She often did.

Judd flung a cumbersome and heavy stack of unassembled boxes that skittered across the floor. Next, he returned with a garbage bag and bubble wrap. "I was trying to straighten up before you got here. You'll feel better once we get some order. I can't handle things if I don't keep busy. Besides, with the fire out there, we've got to protect this stuff."

"Seriously? I get the fire, and yeah, we need to prep for that. We—or I—can do that part fairly quickly. I've done it a thousand times. That goes for his tools, too." She paused to consider what else should be rescued. "Oh, and his notes. Basically, whatever else can't be replaced. Work tables, cabinets, once they're empty, they can stay. I think he'd want the old wheels and probably that jazzy new one. Anyway, like I said, I've done it before. We obviously can't pack the kilns themselves, but we have photos. As long as we've got the important stuff lined up, we're good for now. Packing up anything else might be a little premature. We don't have a clue yet. I'm leaving everything in place until we know what's up."

"Okay, do what you want," Judd muttered.

"Besides," Sage said, "I may be staying on awhile, however things go. The academic life's done me in." She sighed as Judd settled at one of her father's wheels, his boxy frame curled over it. "I need to get a feel for what's up. Just being here and sensing his being helps."

"Get real." This time, it was Judd's voice that hit a higher register. He hated anything that hinted of the supernatural.

Despite her concern, Sage felt drawn to bait him further. Sure enough, he went on. "You don't sense impending disaster? Do you have any concept of logic? Or reality? Like if the wind takes a turn and heads right at us? We'd all turn into crisp cookies."

"Stop babbling and get your butt over here. Let's protect the greenware." Sage pointed to the rows of nearly dry vases. "If we have to hose down the place and any water gets in, we'll have a mud room."

Judd ignored her. He gave the kick wheel a smooth push and stared down as the whirling platform regained its momentum. "By the way, the electric wheel is on its last legs. Needs a new motor, maybe." His attention left the wheel, and the spinning slowed. "Right, and if the roof comes down, we've lost everything."

"It won't. I don't see the fire coming this way, and I don't sense Colin being gone. I mean, really gone." She scowled as Judd gave an exaggerated breath that was meant to sound patient. "Oh, knock it off. You're just like my father—refuses to get into anything he can't see. What I'm telling you feels right."

"That's great if you're into the metaphysical stuff, but that wasn't Colin. I know you haven't been here long. But you eventually need to face it. There's a chance he might be gone." Judd watched her response carefully. "Here's what we know. His canoe is gone. It's off somewhere, but the car is here. He liked to portage. With all the lakes around here, he could have gone anywhere. All we can do is tell folks to watch out for him."

He paused as if to gauge her response.

"You know, Judd, even though I'm worried about his safety, I suppose he could be in some kind of awkward situation, maybe even dangerous. Still, I think the chances are fairly low. Colin always has his protective shield around him." She feigned a scowl and tried to judge how she might taunt Judd a bit more. "Sure, there was the car crash when he was in his thirties, but that was his spirit saving him. And then maybe the worst prospect was Joe coming after him. You know, when he'd gotten a little overly friendly with Joe's wife, and the guy came over here toting a two-by-four." Sage shook her head and crossed her arms. "My mother's powers blocked that danger, and he was okay." *Good grief, he really thinks I mean it.*

She shifted, gazed down at the cup of cold coffee and went on. "He seemed to be afraid of disasters in the studio, but even that always came out all right." She surveyed the massive room. "He never hurt himself lifting things, never had a fire... and hey, I don't think that man ever spilled a drip of slip. And now, I feel like I'm helping protect him as he gets older. Part of my aura looks out for his. I would have done that for Mom too, except with her talents, she wouldn't have been so needy."

Winding up into mystical talk helped Sage break her tension, and it struck her sense of devilishness as well. Judd rolled his eyes, but his calm returned. He wasn't sure where she got her so-called psychic talent, but who cared? If she thought it was bohemian blood from her mother, so what? Or some kind of nymph ancestor. If it was some kind of naive behavior, that was okay, too. How many times had they been through this? He frowned and tried again. "All I'm saying is, it helps to focus on reality, not on the woo-woo stuff."

After countless face-offs, Sage knew his routine. He wasn't much for sticking his neck out, so maybe, at this point, he would simply challenge her to concentrate more on the real world. That was okay.

"If you're always going to latch onto this mystical, gypsy kind of thing, you're never going to come face-to-face with some of the more mature realities of life. You know, you've always been looking for your father in one way or another. You've never been able to 'find' him. No one's truly known him as a person, and that's not going to happen for you, either. Why don't you accept that? Can't you just drop this old woo-woo thing?"

Sage tightened her jaw. How could someone so inherently intelligent also be that clueless? But he'd always been like that. Judd's need for stark reality always came across as an overly harsh way of looking at other people. He tended toward impatience. The glass was always half empty. It was more apparent now that they were older. He wasn't a teenage crush to her anymore. He seemed more like a life impediment. Despite sentiment—and also her delight from goading him—Sage sometimes felt a nearly overwhelming urge to smack him.

His foot moved faster now, and in his place, she imagined her father at the wheel, arms bringing up the sides of a massive vase.

"Could you stop that, please?" The constant whirling made her nerves taut.

"You know how Colin loved women. You saw it, too. He seemed to drink them in. Young, old... well, mostly young. I guess he had a preference for youth—but who doesn't, right?"

She shook her head. "I don't know how he managed to run his summer seminars in North Carolina. He never got in trouble with the powers that be. Still, he used his position and his personality to lure them. He attracted some like flies, but I think others were put off. He had his own rules, and somehow, everyone gave him a pass. I don't know all of what Mom knew, but he never seemed to hide his behavior."

Judd scowled. "How'd that work for you? I never knew what you thought. Wouldn't that hurt your relationship? How'd he just put all that out in front of you?"

"As a kid, I guess I never processed the real depth of it. I didn't see a lot of her pain or anger. She didn't let that much out, and I was too young to process it. Sometimes I felt the tension—or sadness—but she did a great job keeping it from us." Sage took a long breath. "I give them a lot of credit. Together, they always wanted to be good parents. Must have been a challenge. Colin acted like a pretty normal dad— even if he was a bit overly intellectual and free-spirited." She took a long breath as if to collect her thoughts. "It's complicated. I idolized him, and so did the world. It's still the same after all these years. Either I was too young to get it, or maybe I just didn't want to. But I really did—no, I really do—adore him. And I will for all my life. And Mom mostly adored him. Somehow, she managed to separate her feelings from him. I don't understand fully. There's no way I could. Sometimes she seemed very happy, other times not. And there were so many."

"Many happy times?"

"No, many women. Everywhere."

The wheel spun at a breakneck pace as if Judd dared it out of control.

"All right, look. Work here if you want—I know you two have this symbiotic artist thing. But you won't get much done until we know what's up with the fire. And for God's sake, don't move anything around. If we have to close up fast, we need to know where everything is stashed. I have summer and the next semester off. That means I'm not pressured and not on a schedule. I promised Britt she could use the studio for the next few weeks, and I'm not backing out of that—

provided the fire doesn't head for us dead on—then we'd really have to hustle to get stuff out."

* * *

"Hey, kiddo. I didn't realize you'd rented a car." Sage reached out to hug her sister, then looked at the back seat. "Seeing this load, I guess that was a good plan. And I suppose there's more in the trunk?"

Britta laughed and shrugged her shoulders. "How'd you guess? It's pretty full. I decided to pretend I'm a watercolor artist, too. It's a good time of the year for that, and some of the basic designs can work on clay. But hey, any of the seasons up here make for great art."

"You're right. And I guess diversity can be a good thing."

"Actually, I figured I'd rent a car just long enough to get my art stuff up here. Of course, then everything changed. What's the latest on Dad?" She slid a heavy box off the seat and passed it to her sister, who groaned.

Sage sighed. "No news. I know. It's frightening. I'm glad you're here. As you know, two sisters together make three brains." Somehow, a small smile between them seemed to lighten the fear they felt.

"So my buddy Jenna was heading to the Wild West then changed her mind. Now, it's the wild North Shore instead."

"No kidding." Sage struggled to rest the box on her hip. "Sounds like a reasonable plan. But I'm partial to this part of the world anyway. And then what?"

"She'll hang out around Two Harbors for a month or so. Then I'll pick up my stuff and head over there too—like a change of scenery." Britta shrugged her shoulders. "I'll drop off the car up there, and who knows what'll be on the docket next."

Sage continued to wrestle with the box. "How can artist stuff be so heavy?" She struggled to boost it against her hip. "Good grief. What's in here? Rocks? We've got enough geologists meandering around here already."

"Nope, just art supplies. Hey, I'll get that." In one sweep, Britta had the box on a patch of grass near the car.

Sage stood with her arms crossed, trying to look stern. "You

13

realize you'll have to pick that up again later, right? But hey, it looks like you've been weight training anyway. I've got to hustle down to Knife River and the post office. Come along, and we'll see who we can introduce you to. It's only open til 12:30, and I've got some stuff to mail. It's a great place to meet people, and we can start there to show you around."

"Hey, don't make me look like a Martian who just dropped in for the weekend. I grew up here, you know."

"True," Sage said. "It's still a smallish town with great folks—lots of them new since we grew up. Even if your visit is short, I want you to meet them. The post office is a good start. And then," she paused, "for the best part, I want to zip over to Russ Kendall's. You loved that place. Best smoked fish you'll ever taste, and it's been here for a gazillion years."

"Hey, I bet Lake Superior is still there, too."

"You should come home more often," Sage said. "I've missed your faulty sense of humor."

"You bet. How could I forget any of this? When we were kids, we always wanted to see the local action. All those guys down by the river mouth. Woo hoo! Like some kind of ancient revelry. It was the yearly thing—the smelt run! I'll never forget those little silver swimmers. Maybe four inches long? Like the size of skinny Popsicles?"

Sage couldn't hide her laugh. "You got it. And do you remember how those guys—and a few women too—netted them right out of the moving water? It looked like tons of silver, shimmering and flopping into old metal tubs or whatever people had to get them home in. And the ones that got past the nets? Well, they went on, straight into Lake Superior."

"I still remember the smokehouse Grandpa built over behind the garage. He used to settle in and clean those little guys. I suppose it's mostly rotted away by now."

"Sorry to say, Dad had to tear it down. It tilted during a bad storm, and he figured that was a sign." Sage took a long sigh. "Nothing ever stays the same, does it?"

"Well, at least he took pictures."

"Nope. He should have. Maybe that's kind of a guy thing—and we weren't raised by a sentimentalist. At the time, he just wanted to get rid of it. And when all's said, it really could have been a danger to kids—you know, playing down along the lake path. The wind alone could have given it one big wallop."

"Wasn't there something like that in *The Wizard of Oz?*"

* * *

"Oh, good," Judd sighed. "Another struggling artist. That sister of yours has been cruising around here like she owns the place. Was she supposed to be here this soon? Looks like one of those old hippies. Remember? They populated the planet a few decades ago. Every piece of clothes mismatched. At first, I almost didn't recognize her. I think the Doc Martens and that weird costume threw me off."

"I get the picture. Yes, it's Britta. You don't need to go on and on. And by the way, she really does live here." Sounds like she might be going back and forth up the shore.

"God forbid. She's part of this mess?" He flung his arms erratically. "That kid sister of yours could get in the way. Somehow I thought she'd come later in the summer." He took a long breath. " How long has she been here? I didn't see her until a couple days ago."

"Not quite a week. She's been a little lost. Finally went with an art major—but she's one of those older grads who doesn't know where to go next."

"Huh. I suspected that much."

Sage ignored him and went on, "I thought she could stay here and save some money. She liked the idea, and as they say, the rest is history. She's talented, and with Crystal's café being small—really like a little boutique—she wanted unique dinnerware. We thought Britta could make some. And, of course, she warmed up to the idea. Not a bad summer job for a struggling artist, right?"

"Yeah, that's her all right. I've seen her around. She's a little… quirky."

"Sure. Her clothes might be odd, but the tats are pretty well hidden—not that I'm criticizing. But she's got heart. Just a little misdirected right now. She'll focus. And Crystal likes being an art patron."

"Whatever. Just keep her away from me," Judd said. "Give her an area to work in. Like I said. And if that doesn't work, tie her down. Just keep her away from me. And no messing around with my stuff. Got that?"

* * *

The morning started cool, but the Weather Channel had other ideas. Even the North Shore of Lake Superior had summer scorchers. Sage opened the window to give the studio a soothing cross breeze before the temperature started its climb. Today, the ever-present smoke had an almost pleasant smell, like purposeful wisps of piney incense sent her way by a loving forest spirit. She closed her eyes, stretched her head back and slowly inhaled. It was like drifting on a cloud.

Before opening her eyes and slowly exhaling, her senses alerted. She knew he was there, and her body instinctively tightened. Certainly, she'd had that sensation before, but this time it was more urgent. More powerful. A startling chill pulsed through her.

This was clearly not a gentle forest spirit. It was a messenger from hell. There was no positive vibe. Instead, a long-limbed, muscular hulk filled the doorway. Given his face, he definitely was the man in the *Duluth News Tribune*—Holton Denys.

She said nothing while time edged into slow motion. He didn't strike her as a scion of the business world, especially in terms of real estate. Still, his casual lean against the door frame displayed a sense of ownership. She guessed he was more a johnny-come-lately to ventures that might pull in hefty cash without large-scale effort. He was hard to peg and didn't fit her typical classification scheme. Her world mostly included artists like her father and scientists like her colleagues. Despite her wariness, she chose to be cordial—at least initially.

She waited for the next cue. The black and white news photo had disguised his overall visage and body language. In person, the general vibes weren't good. She interpreted the tilt of his head as a sign of excessive arrogance. The next moments would tell her how he used his height, which she estimated to be around six feet. Would he try to use it to intimidate?

"You must be Ms. Soelberg. I thought I'd find you here." His hands pressed against the door frame as if to assess its strength.

She chose to stand, then crossed her arms. "It's Doctor Soelberg. And good morning to you as well." She smiled politely, and he gave a knowing chuckle. There was a metallic coldness about him that made her skin prickle. His smile broadened, and despite his perfect teeth, Sage imagined fangs. His attempt at a power play wouldn't work. She took a step forward in spite of herself. No way would she offer him coffee, and certainly not a chair. By some means she acted, summoning her mother's impatience with self-importance.

"Just came by to look over the place now that you're here. Didn't want to trespass when you weren't around."

She eyed him with a cold stare and fought to suppress a scream of rage. "You're trespassing now." Sage willed her voice not to quaver, but her neck went rigid. More strength, please, she thought.

"Oh, well, technically, that may be," he said. "But how else could I get a good inside look at the place? I wasn't sure you'd be inviting me over anytime soon, and I've got a business to run."

She continued to stare, chin high, fists cocked against her hips. Maybe she felt limp inside, but she sure as hell wasn't going to show it. She could hold this power stance all day if need be. She wanted to snarl, but that would be a bit much.

His eyes darted to the windows, the tall shelves filled with the tools of Colin's life work, the sturdy rafters zig-zagging over the high ceiling. "This open area will make an ideal cocktail lounge... I'm thinking I'll open up the far side, move that wall over on the left, and then enlarge the fireplace." He turned, walked a few paces, scrutinized the rows of metal cabinets, and went on. "Your dad's getting older. Any news on him?"

The shift in perspective was jarring, and she ignored his question. "If and when we ever decide to sell this place—and that's not about to happen, by the way—it won't be to you." Sage picked up a bench knife and smacked its edge hard against the table for emphasis.

Denys gave a slow smile. "Like I said. We never know what's going to happen in our lives, do we? Time could come when you wake up one morning and decide this place no longer fits your needs. Happens all the time. Could happen next week or maybe even tomorrow. Your outlook could change in a minute." He faked an almost fatherly shake of his head.

Sage glanced to the back room, looking to blow off steam. Sure enough, Judd had slipped out, leaving the back door ajar. Wuss. Probably headed for the old boathouse path. A good plan to avoid a verbal skirmish. Maybe he truly feared the man.

"Mr. Denys, if my outlook changes, you can bet you'll be the last to know. And by the way, shouldn't you be busy managing your own business? Last I noticed, your lodge and outbuildings were in the line of fire."

* * *

Crisp, drab leaves crunched as Sage scuffed through them. She turned to look along the drought-ridden trail from the studio to the house. Despite feeling uneasy because of the fire and early falling leaves, she also felt comfort at being home again. There was a feeling of peace and warmth in this place. It must be something in her on-again, off-again psychic makeup that helped clarify the mismatched feelings. Part fear and uncertainty. Yet also somehow revved and electrified.

The smoke seemed less acrid, giving the blanket of shifting haze a deceptively intoxicating aroma. Still, the air carried a stifling heaviness. Along the wooded path back from the shore, there was a distinctive mixture of pine, a mild odor of mud and patches of wet sand.

Along the beach, closer to the water, the sun scorched loose sand and rocks. Maybe the wind had changed slightly, or the fire had reached places where it found less fuel for immediate consumption. There was never a time like this while she was growing up. That thought startled her. She'd never been this close to a fire—even with all her fieldwork—but there were also things she'd never experienced. The odd and awful sense of dread. The fear of something she couldn't fathom. A sense of unknowing that gripped her heart. Was the burning in her eyes the precursor of tears or simply the sting of smoke? While fate might have the chance to destroy her father, the fire certainly had the ability to destroy her world in a way just as terrifying. Who could say which was worse? She shuddered in the warm sunshine, yet the tips of her fingers were cold and numb.

* * *

Great luck, Judd thought to himself. It was inevitable she'd come back. After all, her father was missing. But now the timetable was totally screwed. He flipped the knife and caught it in his hand. Tossed and caught it again, then exhaled a spew of smoke. So much for quitting. Sure, it rotted your lungs, but the white powder was a less comforting alternative.

He could rearrange the shelves. Colin's absence, along with the fire, was a good excuse. How a brick of heroin could disappear eluded him. But it was his mistake. He'd been sure he was the only one working in the studio. But then Britta came along. Damn. Not only was she a huge headache, but if someone else found out, who knew what would happen? For sure, it would still be there now. He just hadn't had enough time to move everything. Terror gnawed at his stomach. It was doubtful it would be missed from the larger stash right away. But if word got out that it had been found—as it surely would—and where—he'd likely be dead. Dead in the water like a couple other poor fools he'd known. Ankle weights were for physical training, not for swimming. He'd have to come back at night. Maybe bring Frank, his old buddy. As usual, the guy would be a pain in the ass…the kind who would think up some kind of bizarre cut for his trouble. Who'd think a brick now and then would be missed? Or had they been watching him all along?

Judd's shirt stuck to his chest, and his pants chafed in all the wrong places. Laundry was a task he hadn't considered recently. Probably wouldn't happen any time soon, either. Though the temperature was comfortable, he was not. His whole body felt out of sorts. Stress? Could be, but he wasn't the type to just move to another task. Might be just the pure hate that boiled up in him. But still, there was a feeling of relief that perhaps his nemesis—whoever it might be—could be vanquished. Annihilated and out of his life forever. The guy deserved it. Too bad he'd have to die, though. But he couldn't take chances. It would be a while before they found him, and by then, he'd be on his way. Hard to imagine living anywhere else, but with his score evened, it was time to find a new life. He'd stashed enough away to make the transition reasonably smooth. And that asshole Denys would find him work elsewhere—along with the right paperwork for a new identity. With his background, change was inevitable. But he'd always managed to evade it. Now he anticipated it as embracing a new life—one where he was master, and no one could screw him again. Like moving up the career ladder. And damn it, he deserved it for what he and his mother had gone through. But that wouldn't happen if they found out his hand had been in the till.

* * *

The phone broke Alex's concentration. When he bolted, so did his beer. "Yeah, Jax." He moved quickly to sop up the liquid creeping toward his laptop. "No. Working on it now. Give me thirty—I'll get back." Jackson was an impatient partner.

While wiping the table, Alex's thoughts returned to the woman he'd seen that morning at the post office. Word had it that she was a little quirky. Great, just great. That's all he needed. He'd assumed from his minimal research that she was an airhead who thought she was some kind of bohemian and was probably into seances. No Facebook page or website. Did that mean she was some kind of nonconformist or maybe just very private? He wiped the wet beer bottle with his already damp sweatband and took a swig. Even the brew seemed to have a faint smoky taste.

Earlier that day, she'd walked past his Jeep and into the post office. Filthy khakis. Stained blue work shirt with brown splotches. What, deck stain? Spilled coffee? Maybe a trip under some kind of rattle scrap vehicle?

Black hair? Or maybe just dark brown? Longish, caught in a ponytail and pulled through the elastic a few times, making it bend back over itself. Feet trapped in rundown mocks. A Minnesota thing? He had second thoughts about using her for cover. Following her into the post office could be a stupid move, particularly if he wanted to get a good look. Hell, that would really screw his reputation. And the entire investigation. It was also dubious—no, make that insane—a rookie? And someone who wouldn't even know she was part of the plan—even if just for cover? Sounded like a bad TV movie.

Pondering his next so-called assignment was one thing. But given what he knew about the current mess, the effort could backfire—big time. He'd learned to pay attention to that feeling. There were some missions he wished he could forget. As he toyed with the alternatives, his thoughts moved from the post office parking lot back to his office chair. Okay, option A. He drew a blank. Well then, B. What was B? He straightened in his chair and cranked up Elvis. Hell, he didn't even know what his options were, and the room was closing in. He stepped outside and inhaled the smoky night, blew pretzel crumbs off his phone, then dialed. "Hey. I need your head."

* * *

Back from Colorado, one of Sage's first visits was to her friend Crystal at Loonatic's. She'd heard from friends that the new restaurant was prospering.

"Fabio, you stay outside. I'm thinking in Minnesota we might have a law about dogs wandering around inside restaurants. If you were wearing your tux, it might be a different story." The golden retriever whined, then stretched out on the warm sidewalk by the door. "Good boy. Maybe our friend Crystal will have a treat for you when we leave, okay?" There was a snort as Fabio turned his head away from her. "Well, okay. Be like that. Supper's a long way off."

The dining room at Loonatic's was nearly empty after a respectable lunch clientele. The restaurant's specialty items, "Northwoods cuisine with a Dixie touch," had caught on, and the day's blackened walleye club sandwich was a winner. The clink of flatware from behind the swinging doors was a reassuring melody to the establishment's owner, Crystal Yarborough. As their friendship grew, Sage learned how

21

Crystal's childhood and culture had shaped a completely different frame of reference. No wonder lifestyles in the north—especially in northern Minnesota—sometimes baffled her.

"You've done a great job with this," Sage said. "I was hoping for your success, but wow! I didn't expect it this soon. I can't believe you've been in Minnesota for such a short time, and yet—snap! Instant tourist impact."

"Blah, blah, blah. Wow, y'all sound like that restaurant reviewer I met the other day. You'll give me a big head," Crystal laughed. "I know I'm not ready for four stars, but I'd be ecstatic with three." She moved past the bar with hands on her hips. "Not that bad for a wily runaway wife, right? That nasty fool of a husband might figure out Minnesota is north of the Gulf, but beyond that, he'd never expect me to be out in the woods. I set this up so it'd be pretty hard to find me. And if he does, I've got a whole bunch of protectors lined up at the bar."

An afternoon break with Crystal was the best relief Sage could wish for. Although stressed from her encounter with Holton Denys, she already felt the strain lifting. The two settled at a round table near the bar, both folding napkins and making sure the wine glasses gleamed to perfection.

"Okay, I'll lay off the compliments. What I really came for is some gossip. What do you know about Holton Denys?" Sage rubbed a towel over the rim of a wine glass. "Lipstick doesn't come off easily, does it?" She set the glass aside. "He wants our place and stops just short of threatening me. Talk about pressure."

"Developers are always aggressive. Don't turn your head, but that's his right-hand guy at the bar. Alex Rogers." Crystal nodded in his direction. "Word is Denys hired him as a kind of go-between and PR person. You know, to soothe the community. He just looked over here."

"Is he watching now? Can I look?" Sage turned, propped an elbow and held a nonchalant, sideways slouch to get a better view. "He reminds me of the Marlboro Man from the old cigarette ads. Remember how he used to sit rough and ready on his horse?" She leaned back and gave a quiet laugh. "I'd know him on the street anywhere." He stared back, pushed from the bar and stood to his full height. About what she'd guessed. "Oh, great. He's headed this way. Now what?"

Crystal shrugged her shoulders. "Relax, girl. Take a deep breath. I'll use my Southern wiles on him." She usually had good advice, but sometimes it seemed overplayed.

He sauntered to the table, then extended his hand to Sage. "You're the geologist? Or archaeologist? Must be hard to do your job with that inferno headed toward us."

"Yes and no. I'm taking a break right now—back here to settle some family business. I didn't expect to stumble into all this chaos."

He turned to Crystal. "And you serve Southern food here?"

"Some. But you don't think our red beans combined with Minnesota wild rice sound like Dixie, do you?"

He laughed and turned toward Sage. His handshake was firm and long. "Alex Rogers, with HDE… that's Holton Denys Enterprises."

Sage fixed her gaze on him with what she realized must be an ill-tempered stare.

Alex looked back calmly. He'd been trained to observe rather than make quick judgments. "Beg your pardon?"

"Sorry. No problem. My mind wanders," she said, attempting to sound slightly bored. His straightforward manner caught her off guard.

Crystal interrupted and let her imagination take over. "Sage is a sage. She's been meditating. Sometimes, she goes into a trance."

He blinked, his grin reflecting amusement. One eyebrow arched up.

Sage jumped in. "Anyway, So you're the front man for Denys? The PR guy? Or is it real estate advisor? Along with translator of local customs?" She added a pause for effect. "Henchman?"

"Actually, I don't get into real estate, but the others? Yeah, I guess you nailed it."

"But you're here to talk me out of my family property, right? Forget it. Your employer has already wheedled himself into this community—and we've caught on. He's got property right now on what used to be a prime piece of land."

"Still is a prime piece of land."

"Not anymore. And don't talk to me about local jobs. We don't want them."

"Looks like there are a few people out here who could use them. In case you haven't noticed, the boom times are over for this area. If people want to stay, there's got to be a reason other than sentiment." He felt irritation taking over. "Oh, and speaking of sentiment, I heard about your father's disappearance. Any developments?"

"No news. We don't know if there was…" Sage's throat caught, and her voice faded. Why was she answering? "Actually, we don't know anything. But we're sure he's fine."

"Lots of big lakes."

Sage curled her fists and struggled for control as she stood from her chair. "Stay away from me and my property. Tell your boss that, too." There was a long pause. She realized the talk had come to a dead stop.

"Well, ladies, I've got work to do." Alex's grin came straight from the devil. He sauntered toward the door, then turned. "That your husky out front?"

"You mean Fabio."

"Yeah. The dude with two eye colors? Kind of spooky. He's been sitting in the middle of the sidewalk the whole time. Wouldn't let me by until I shook with him." He gave Fabio a grin. "Looks like he could be a real handful. Like my baby sister used to say, looks like he's smarter than his brains."

* * *

One of the pleasures of home meant retracing steps and revisiting her childhood: walking the ageless trails, cruising rutted roads, checking on neighbors and friends, wondering if pebbles she'd flung into streams had been carried away to faraway places.

Colin's studio had been alive at night, not always with artistic endeavor but with father-and-daughter activities. A young Sage absorbed nature lessons, music and deep philosophical discussions. Other children were satisfied merely watching television.

Night always drew Sage outdoors, even if there was little visible moon to enjoy. How many times had she scampered barefoot down that path as a little girl? In her joy to explore the woods, she'd made a loopy series of trails, crisscrossing and stretching back and around the studio and house. It was a maze she knew well, with a few devious hiding places along the way. A meandering byway led to the ravine, where she'd carefully placed rocks to serve as a camouflaged series of steps.

On this night, clouds partially covered the moon, making for a dark night. Sage saw an outdoor light shining by the studio door. Must've forgotten it earlier.

Sure in her memory that cemented the way, she whistled for Fabio, then headed along the path, striding toward the faint studio light that flickered through the tamaracks. Despite the fire, the air felt damp and heavy, and mist hung around the studio door. She turned her face upward to inhale the smoky yet sweet night air as her dog trotted ahead.

The peace was interrupted by a kind of grasping, clawing hush. Even Fabio seemed to notice. He gave a short whine and stopped several times along the path, lifting his nose as if to detect an unusual scent. He gave a low growl.

Something hard and ragged smashed between Sage's shoulder blades. She flew forward, landing on her face and palms. As she scrambled to rise, a fist-sized rock struck her neck. She responded with a side kick that apparently landed where she only dared hope. Her attacker screamed and cursed. It was not a familiar voice.

Grasping opportunity while ignoring her own agony, Sage flung her upper body toward a hidden side path. The small light by the door brought pure luck. It allowed Sage to maneuver but was useless to the intruders. She heard Fabio's furious barking through a jungle of shrubs, then in a more open area near the stream bed. Her breathing was ragged. Still, she willed her rubber legs toward the dry ravine with its branches and hidden paths.

As she neared solid ground, the sole of her sandal caught a rock. Her upper body flew forward, leaving the rest behind. She was airborne again before thudding onto gravel. Surely, they'd pick up her location. Barely moving, Sage edged her body behind a winding debris pile from the last flood. She grasped small, quiet breaths and waited. Was there a breeze, or did her body sense the chill of something else? She crept forward in the underbrush while the footsteps circled around her. Judged by whistles from two directions, she hoped there were only two people. How much time had passed? She struggled to rise, if only for a limited view. The sound of her gasping, then breathing, then gasping, startled her. Covering her mouth, she felt the wet stickiness of blood on the palm of her hand.

A light bobbed. Flashlight. She heard thrashing through the thicket and the sound of rustling weeds somewhere behind her. The image of a sharp scythe whipping through the underbrush streaked through her mind. Fabio ran ahead, his bark coming first from the right, then from behind on the left, then back into the woods.

The beam ahead continued to bounce through leaves and brush, sometimes upward or now and then scanning in wide sweeps. Someone was trying to sweep around and through the trees. At her? Yes. She looked for a lower part of the ravine. The beams swooped and dipped like frantic fireflies.

The path was brittle and harsh without her sandals, and thorns slapped and scraped across her face. Faster. But stay quiet. Stay down. Her left foot slipped on wet grass, and trying to stay upright, she jammed her right hand on a rock protruding from the ravine wall. Muffling a squeal of pain, she kept to the safety of the dry stream bed, no longer daring to peer through the brush above.

The light kept coming. They would certainly find her. Her palm throbbed, and she struggled again to control her breath, for fear panting would give her away. Rustling came from at least two directions. Was Fabio nearby? Were there more than two people? Or was it two plus one dog? Then came bursts of random movement back and forth, apparently ripping through branches and underbrush. That must be Fabio. She hoped again he would lead them away from her. But what if they had weapons?

They seemed closer. Could they hear her heart pounding? With the partly hidden moon, she felt safer—unless the clouds broke. She had no intention of moving. She still heard thrashing in the bushes and, once in a while, a hint of a slight whisper. Were they keeping their voices down so she wouldn't recognize them? She hadn't heard any dog cries for help. He must be safe. Maybe lying in wait.

Eventually, the sounds faded, and judging by rustling along the paths, two people came together in the distance. Sage detected disjointed mumbling and finally silence as the movement became more distant.

Time was deceptive, and the night seemed to grow even darker. She felt as if she'd been motionless for hours, silently waiting for any change in the sounds and air around her. The stillness was colder now, and she tightened her jaw to stop the urge to chatter. How much was cold, and how much was adrenalin?

She had no intention of moving. Where was she now? Was she above the ravine or still in it? She realized it wasn't the path she was on or even the overhang near the top of the ravine. She was south of the studio. As she restored her bearings, her panic waned. That feeling alone helped her feel safer—and surely no one could follow her frenzied escape.

Where was Fabio? She knew he was too smart to lead anyone to her. So she waited, gradually easing from her crouched position and extending her legs. The sand felt oddly comforting. She pressed her body into it, resting as quietly and easily as the night allowed. Her legs itched incessantly, and she fought not to scratch. The night wore on while the wind picked up. Either she was totally exhausted or simply so shattered by terror that it didn't matter. It blew above her, whistling and swirling over the dry stream bed.

* * *

Morning came before she dared move. A dreamlike state surrounded her. Get out of the ravine. Take the higher path that runs up from the crest. Breathe deeper. She imagined herself crawling. Where's Fabio? Don't worry—he knows where you are. Okay, no sound, just lie flat. The creeps are gone. No, what's that? A wild animal?

"Fabio!"

The dog's tail made wide sweeps against her leg, and from above the ravine, she heard a voice—one remotely familiar.

27

"Sage! You down there? You all right?"

In her painful stupor, she groaned and put her arms around the dog. "Oh, Fabio, you noodlehead. I love you so much."

Her head felt as if slammed on bricks, and her entire frame had a disembodied feel. A sort of floating detachment. She groaned.

"Don't move, I'm coming down. Stay where you are. It's okay."

The voice brought a strange recollection. Could it be the guy from Crystal's bar? Alex Rogers? The guy who worked for Holton Denys? What could he possibly be doing here? But she wasn't ready to move anyway. She tried to edge up on one elbow, but every fiber in her body fought back. Fabio sat close, waiting. If he thought the guy was okay, she would be okay.

"God, not you again," she slurred. Exhaustion and pain had nearly taken her ability to speak.

"Okay, let me know if you need anything. I can swing by later." He scowled down at her. The pause was long, and Sage started to drift. "Well, maybe I came on a little strong the other day."

"More like an ass," she said. Her words faded into a prolonged sigh. She tried to look up the bank, but exhaustion took over.

"And you?" Alex asked. "Anyhow, I was headed down the main road—rented the old Glascoe cabin about a mile back—and your dog, he just sat in the middle of the blacktop and howled. Not very smart. I needed to get him out of there. I know dogs, and we were already friends. He howled a couple times. Clearly, there was a problem. Took us a while to get on each other's wavelength, but he wanted me to follow. So, I pulled onto the shoulder, parked the car and off we trekked. And here I am. What the hell happened to you?"

"At least two goons decided to play kickball with me. I was less into the game, as you can see." She raised her head, and he saw the bruises and blotches on her face, arms and legs.

"Good God. What did you get into? You're pretty black and blue. Let's hope the rest of you isn't covered with poison ivy."

"Got into? I'm not sure. It might have something to do with your boss," Sage said. Given her current situation, she had no desire for small talk with one of Denys's henchmen. On the other hand, politeness might be the best approach. The thought of getting out of an unstable stream bank on her own wasn't pleasant. Besides, she might learn something. "I'm better than last night. Back then, I was moving any way I could, and it shows." She recalled her brushes with loose rocks and biting insects.

"Are those bites? From sand flies?"

"Probably what we backwoods folks call no-see-ums. Can't see 'em, but they pack a major bite." Sage squirmed in an effort to sit up.

"Hey! Not so fast. Let's check you out first." He had her move her legs and arms. "Can you sit up?"

"I think so. I'm fine. Really."

"The hell you are." He started down the bank sideways, sometimes sliding and other times using his feet to step from rock to rock—making sure not to send loose rock and debris in her direction.

She stood. Slowly. With Alex partly pushing and sometimes nearly dragging her, their progress to solid ground seemed endless. "I need to be back in Colorado by early September," Sage groaned.

"No worries. I'm pretty sure we'll have you on higher ground at least by late August."

When they reached the top, they rested. "Now. Can you walk? I found your sandals. They were by that scraggy part. Like where the weeds start to meet the sand." He tipped his head toward the edge of the stream bank. "Let's see your foot... no big gashes. Put them on for now. Walk slowly, and we'll clean you up when we get back."

"Back? We? And where?"

He held her arm while Fabio whined. "It's okay, boy. We've got her now." He ran a hand over the dog's head. "You're a good boy. Lots of treats for you when we get back."

* * *

Sage pointed Alex toward the house, where he found towels and first aid supplies. Purple welts and insect bites on her face and arms confirmed a rough night in the woods. The soles of her feet had mostly escaped major cuts, but bruises made walking painful. Nasty scrapes ringed her ankles and crossed the tops of her feet. Her hair was matted and tangled. Scuffs of dirt on her elbows and jeans suggested a slide down the slope to the dry creek bed.

"I'll grab a pillow, and we can prop your feet on the coffee table."

He strode to the closest bedroom. Definitely Sage's room. It was a mish-mash of decades. Artwork from grade school occupied shelves with books on Pompeii and ancient Greece. A framed child's painting of a lighthouse standing on a high cliff. The one just up the shore? Not bad, he decided. Somehow, it reminded him of Picasso.

A rock hammer and field notebooks rested on a side table, along with an aging Brunton compass. No, not just an antique, but more like a relic from ages past. He wondered if she'd sell it to him. He could check prices in his spare time. He recalled he didn't have spare time.

Good grief, there was Barbie wearing a black and white striped swimsuit and lounging on a flat piece of sandstone. Clever. A few inches away was a small, carved music box. Maybe it served as a radio for the sunbathers. Alex felt lost in time.

"Hey. You get lost in there?" Sage sounded impatient.

"Can you shower by yourself?"

"Yeah. Been doing it for years."

Interesting, he thought. She wasn't keen on getting help, particularly from him.

"Sorry, I'm really beat," Sage said.

"Don't go soft on me now. Shower first, then we'll take a closer look at your feet. Better to get the worst crud off without rubbing it in."

"We?"

"You bet. Once we can see past the dirt, we'll cover up the bigger scrapes, so they stay clean."

As he guided Sage carefully from the sofa, Alex spoke slowly and quietly to Fabio. "It's okay, big boy. Don't worry. Everything's okay. You don't have to whine."

He looked at Fabio's one blue eye and one brown eye. "I do like that you're so flexible with eye colors. Wasn't sure at first— but those eyes are great for an undercover sleuth." He reached down to scratch the dog's head, then noted, "Blue. For today I'd go with the blue. It's more piercing in case we stumble onto some thugs. Or intense, if you will. And you do want to be intense, don't you, my boy? Just remember to turn that side of your head toward the villains." Alex stepped back for a long look. "And then around here, let's go for the brown. That way, you'll look more—mellow—you know?"

Fabio responded with another whine.

"And don't worry, big guy. Your mom'll be fine."

Whoa. He pointed at Sage's arm. "Looks like a snag from barbed wire. When was your last tetanus shot?"

"You expect me to remember that now? I can hardly recall my name."

"Right. We should check." Alex rolled his sleeves. "Do you have sweatpants? That way, we can hike up the legs while we take care of the mess around your feet. Get along, now."

"Wait. I'll never get these jeans off—I might as well cut them."

"I'll help."

"The hell you will."

"Okay, look. Just tell me where the sweats are. If I close my eyes and brace you, you can cut down. And slowly, please. We want to keep dirt out of those scrapes."

"Right, okay. Sweats in the closet. Kitchen scissors in the drawer by the sink," she said. "I can't bend down to my feet. They're still smudged—like the dirt is permanent. There's no seeing how bad they are." She tried bending for a closer look, then recoiled in pain.

"Over there," he waved toward the bathroom. "Just take a normal shower if you can. Swish your feet around."

"You think that'll help?"

"It'll get most of the grime off first. That's why I got the basin." He led her to the bathroom, and she got in the shower.

* * *

Fabio gave a sharp bark and dropped to the floor.

"What's that you're saying, Fabio? You think he's okay? All right. If you say so, maybe I'll trust him a little—very little."

"Cut me some slack, will you? I know you're worried about your father, and I know last night was hell, but…" Alex knelt, held her foot and

31

turned it slightly, looking for areas of broken skin. Despite leaving a trace of dirt on her feet, the shower had revived Sage's spirits, if only slightly. She seemed more open to talking, even if that included grilling him.

"I hear you've been cozying up to the folks around here," she said. "Some are keeping an eye on you. What's that about?"

"I'm new here. Just doing my job. You knew that when we first met, right?"

"Well, yes. But what's this game you're playing?"

"No game. Just trying to be a good neighbor while I'm here."

"Oh, please." Sage gave an exasperated sigh. "These are honest, straightforward folks. Don't be messing with their heads."

"I wouldn't think of messing heads." He paused for a moment, trying to match his brain with his speech.

Sage tried not to laugh. "Sounds like you're a little rattled right now. Are you? Maybe I need to call the police." A good ploy, she thought. She tried to spring from the sofa, but Alex held her back. There was a long silence as he glared at the floor.

"Shit." He slowly looked up from her feet. "I *am* the police. Just like any other cop. Well, not exactly. I have a reputation for being a one man army. I'm *like* the police. Sort of. Crap." Had he really just said that? "I'm faster and a lot closer at hand."

"A little rattled are you? Police? That's a lie. You either work for Denys or you're with the government." She was silent for what seemed like a very long moment.

"Hold on. I…"

"Give it up. Right now, I'd be a fool to trust you for much of anything." She was silent for what seemed like a very long moment. A derisive laugh escaped her lips. "Am I right?" She jerked her foot back, and water splashed from the basin.

"No."

Sage scowled and poised her foot for another splash.

"Take it easy! You're going to resist now? Now that you're safe from those goons you managed to pick up?"

"I have no idea if I'm safe. I'm baffled about what you're doing. But I don't have the time or energy to get tied up with you—or any of your other idiots—by accident."

"Look. You'll play by my rules. Either cool it and keep your mouth shut, or head back West. What'll it be?"

"I came back to find my father. Nothing's changed. That's my agenda. Period." She stomped her foot in the basin, then raised it, sending soapy water over his shirt and into his face.

"Knock it off, damn it, or I'll bring you down right along with that band of crooks." He paused, then took slow, deep breaths. "Sorry. I can get pretty nasty. Most of the time, I come across as fairly normal. I've been quite laid back over the last day or so. And by the way, it looks like you have a bit of a hair-trigger attitude, too, right?"

After a few more breaths, his demeanor changed. Although she barely knew the man, she sensed he'd finally gone off duty for the day.

"Sorry." He exhaled. "I can get pretty wound up sometimes."

Sage wasn't sure how much of Alex's spewing was real or simply frustration. When she and her sister got out of hand, Colin used to send them off to their rooms. Not something one could do with Alex.

"I'll tend to my business," Sage said. "You do yours… whatever that is. Looks to me like you've exhausted yourself, Mr. Macho."

"Pretty close. Hell. I feel like I'm in the middle of a spaghetti Western. Except I don't have enough energy to be funny."

"You seem to be a clever cop—or whatever you are." Sage struggled for words. "What do you do when someone gets in the way? This is the wilderness, not the big city. I can't take back-to-back violence."

"You need to keep your mouth shut. Do you get that? No one hears about any of this. Not even your friend at the bar. And the less *you* know, the better."

"Restaurant. Not bar. And I need Crystal's help."

How had he single-handedly managed to blow his cover? An asinine mistake. A rookie blunder. He wanted to rewind the whole conversation—if that's what you'd call it. People usually followed his orders—especially women. But this time, his demand was hopeless. "Screw things up for me, and we're both dead."

"Seriously?"

"Oh, yeah. Seriously. Now put your foot down."

"You'd be a good nurse," Sage said, looking for a good way to clear the air.

To his surprise, she sunk back into the sofa. Exhaustion could be a good thing. In fact, maybe he could use it to redirect their conversation. "Sage. Interesting name."

"We're not done with this, you know."

He pressed ahead. "Your parents wanted a child full of wisdom?"

"That's what my father took it for—and what my mother let him believe. But actually, she was into herbs. I think she was going for a name that expressed a sort of smoothness, yet a little rough around the surface. Like Sage. Probably like she wished she was."

"And now you're feeling caught between what?"

"Something like that, I guess." She frowned again. "Think you're pretty perceptive, don't you?"

"Yeah, sometimes I surprise myself," Alex said.

"This water's getting cold."

"Okay, princess, hang on." Back in the kitchen, he held the basin under hot water. "See how this feels." He returned to gently massage her foot, and she closed her eyes.

"Your stomach's growling. You should eat something. What's in your refrigerator?"

"I suppose some tofu—that's mine—and maybe some cheese. Probably stale bread. He usually tosses it out for the birds, and it doesn't last long. If there's a lot out there, he hasn't been gone long."

She lowered her head, trying to think. "And hey—we know when he went shopping with MT." She tried to piece together a timeline. "Oh. And there would be beer. I'm thinking maybe a couple six packs."

"Wouldn't he take that with him?"

"Doubtful. He'd probably say it intruded on nature."

"Let's finish here, and I'll rustle something up. Hold your foot out. This part looks worse than I thought." He rubbed again with his thumb, making circular motions between her toes and over the bottom of her foot while her head dropped, and she sighed. The turquoise nail polish was odd, and it brought him once again to the Mediterranean with its nearly surreal blue-green water. A crazy thought and one he tried to shake.

"Ouch." Her cry brought him back to the present.

34

"Sorry. There's a little cut. Let me get plenty of soap on it, then we'll cover it. There's a nasty one on the top of your foot, too, but it won't bother your walking."

"No big deal. I've cut myself more than once. It gets hard to always wear heavy shoes in the desert heat."

"You're going to check on the tetanus shot, right? Soon?"

She nodded and took a long breath, perhaps a signal that sleep wasn't far off.

"There. It's not as bad as I thought." He finished dabbing her clean feet with a towel, then pressed down the corner of a small adhesive pad. "Got any white socks? They'd be best with the scrapes and cuts. And maybe some looser shoes? Sandals aren't the best right now."

"Top left drawer for the socks, and there are some old scuffs—probably under the bed."

He inched the socks on.

She settled into the soft leather of her father's Scandinavian recliner, and he watched her feet rise. "Rest now," he said. He noticed what looked like a genuine smile.

"Just… thanks." Sage exhaled a long breath, then slept.

* * *

It was late afternoon before she stirred. He had slept, too. The sense of exhaustion left him limp and numb.

He dropped to the floor next to the recliner, rested his arms on his knees and looked up at Sage. "I've got to get out of here. It's the approach of claustrophobia. Can you make it if we move outside?"

"Not a bad idea."

Sage found an aging army blanket in the garage along with battered boat cushions. They reminded her of backyard tea parties she staged with her sister Bridget. The boys down the road had no interest in tea parties. Years later, Sage hid the dishes in her bedroom closet, saving them from a trip to Goodwill.

Bending down was easier than earlier, and her spirits rose. Alex settled across the worn blanket and raised his feet on a boat cushion.

"Why do you call your father Colin?"

"That's his name."

"I get that," Alex said. "But why not Dad, or Pops, or something normal?"

"Because he wasn't—isn't——like a dad or a pops."

"I'm guessing you're close to him. Like you have a relationship most kids would envy."

"For sure. But that doesn't make him anything like a typical father. He's more like..." she paused, trying to find a good description. "In some ways, he's more like a friend. A buddy. Other times, like a teacher." She looked at Alex to judge his reaction. "He used to make up special games in his studio." She thought about how unusual her father was and how her friends were envious. "At the same time, he was what you'd call a normal father. Like nonstop love, protection— and stern when he needed to be."

"I'm getting an interesting picture of you and your dad," Alex said. "You have a sister, right? I hate to ask, but were you the favorite?"

"No, not really." She paused for a moment. "I guess it might look that way, but it's not. It's more that one kid's personality is more like the mother, and a sibling seems to connect more with their father."

"So what about your life together as a family?"

"When Dad went away for summer pottery sessions, I think Mom wanted to show him that we girls—that's what she called us—could go off on our own too. Britta, my sister, was always ready to hit the road. That feeling has stuck with her as long as I can remember. When Dad packed his van, we grabbed our sleeping bags and piled into Mom's old pickup. Believe me, it was crowded. We three all squashed into the front seat, and she had one of those things like a roof that covered the open part in the back. There was just enough room for our sleeping bags. I don't remember ever getting cold at night. Anyway, Colin headed for an old lodge in North Carolina—they used it as a student dorm for summer." She stretched back her head and sighed as if to think more clearly. "Meanwhile, we had no idea where we were headed. Usually, it was toward Minnesota farm country. At night, we could smell the damp fields."

She waited for Alex to laugh, but he didn't.

"Sometimes we camped in churchyards, but if we couldn't find one, we looked for old farm roads. The best ones had deep ditches and tall corn. If we scrunched down, our sleeping bags kept the bugs off. One time, there was a 4H ballfield, and the farm kids asked us to play. When the mist rolled in, we edged away and pulled out our gear. When the game broke up and the elders rushed to the tavern, it was dark enough for us to claim the ditches. The scent of mowed hay hid the smell of our bug spray, and the ditch felt as good as my bed at home. The crickets chirped, and I saw a buck across the ballfield. I pretended to be a doe who would wake up at sunrise and leave my shape in the grass."

Alex scanned the cloudy sky. "You were lucky to have a partly cloudy sky last night—even though you caught it cloudless now and then."

"And the spirits were active." She grinned at him and wondered how far she could go with her paranormal talk.

"You're a scientist, right? Cut the act, all right?"

She grinned. "Which part? The scientist or the act?"

"Just cut the paranormal crap."

She shrugged. "Keeps me from getting too serious. Don't tell anyone, but I have a tendency for that."

"But why do you spew that crap? Do you believe it?"

"Aside from driving Judd—and apparently you—crazy? I do get a kick out of pondering life from more than one perspective. But seriously, it gives me a broader way to think. No, it's a way of thinking. Like going with what comes at you. Saying 'well, maybe' before tossing it aside? Give it a chance! Maybe something new or exciting or wonderful is ready to just pop into your life."

Alex huffed. "Like that crazy romp you had in the woods last night? Or maybe the killer forest fire of a lifetime?"

"Not really. But I do like thinking in different ways. Turning reality on its head. In a way, it fits with archaeology. Look at some of the ancient cultures, the ideas they believed—ones we might think were weird or downright crazy." There was no response from Alex, so she went on. "I like to fit some of those into the way I look at life. I trust the science part, and thinking in broader circles adds a different perspective."

"You do sound like a professor."

"Is that boring? Maybe, I guess. But I got hooked. My mother was always attracted to the idea of wood nymphs. I guess some hung out in groups, and others were more solitary. Those tales excited her and led her to her own desire to take off to travel whenever she liked. Like that story I told you about how we slept in ditches on our road trips. As I got older, I realized those nomadic trips may have been a kind of escape from her life with Colin."

Sage was quiet for a moment, as if replaying life in her head. "Back when I was a kid, both of them liked to entertain me with their creative stories. Someone in the family told my mother we had nymph relatives that hung out in trees. Not such a good habitat for them in the midst of a major forest fire, right?"

Alex groaned and stretched his legs. "Okay. Starting tomorrow— provided you can walk—we're going to start sorting this out. My way. That way, we ignore the wood nymphs for now. I need you to meet Jax. That's Jackson, my partner, and I want you to talk with your friend— Crystal? God help us, she'd better be halfway sane. Like I said, the less you know, the better. I'll spell out some of the basics, and we need to have an understanding. If your father ties into that, so be it. But we're doing things my way. My priority is investigating—and nailing—Holton Denys. And by the way, you're not staying here alone tonight."

"Fine with me. You're worried one of the wayward wood nymphs might stop by?"

"One more thing." Alex bent toward her, either to make sure she was listening or to force his point. "I don't play by the book."

* * *

Thursday dawned with a slight breeze carrying a hint of smoke. Given the wind direction, it could be a reasonably tolerable day. Sage was wary to return to the stream bed—or anywhere near it. Yet, given the circumstances, it seemed she didn't have a choice. With Alex in the lead, they struck out to retrace her steps.

She knew he was coaxing her to relive details. Where was she when the attack began? What did she hear? Could she sense any shuffling in the drier, sandy areas? Could she tell boots from shoes? Did she hear crunching sounds over stones? Had she seen vegetation near the dry stream bed? Or larger rocks? Markers like that could help pin down the location. Could she sense footsteps on small stones? Like the crunching from boots or shoes? Or did other stones—say, stones the size of golf balls—clack together?

Was there any talking? Was she sure they were both men? Yes, not unless there was a woman with a baritone voice. Did one give orders while the other followed? It was hard to tell, but she recalled the sound of a whistle. Was that some kind of signaling? Was she absolutely sure there had only been two people? Could there have been a third person across the stream bed? Good grief, was he even going to know if she heard them spit on the rocks?

How close did the thugs come to her? Was she able to get any kind of fix about where both those jackasses were? Were they covering separate areas? There was a yell of sorts. Had one been injured? Clearly, it wasn't an ankle, or they wouldn't be able to flee quickly. Were they close enough to hear even the slightest of her movement? God help her if she'd sneezed. Did she hear shuffling around the brush? Through it? Could she tell if anyone had scraped a branch and left blood behind? If she heard voices, could she nail them down again? His questions seemed endless, and some nearly absurd. Good grief, she thought. Did he want to know if they were breathing or what cologne they were wearing?

After firing endless questions, Alex seemed to ponder. Over and over, his eyes darted from the stream bed into the brush.

"I'm guessing your thugs weren't familiar with the path. Looks like someone took a flier right here—or was that you?" He pointed to skid marks over bent weeds and underbrush.

"Nope. Not me. When I fell, I was careful to hit sand and gravel so I'd scrape lots of skin off." She paused. "Hey, you're supposed to laugh at that."

"Right. Are your psychic powers telling you anything?" The mocking brought a sneer from Sage.

"Only that you're a macho guy with a short-term memory." She followed the sarcasm. "I thought we'd clarified that. But let's try again.

Of course, I'm not really psychic—I'm highly perceptive. And I've learned to trust my gut. It helps in the tough decisions, you know. You ought to try it." She dropped onto a rotting log that stretched over the ravine. "Need to adjust my shoe."

"Probably time for a rest anyway. You're not a hundred percent yet." He settled on the edge of rock.

"We're polar opposites," she went on. "You're rigid. Kind of lost in your head. But if it helps, you can call me psychic. I'll go with it. Cerebral might be more accurate. So, what was going on when you drifted away yesterday? You were lost in your head somewhere. It was crazy."

He sat silent, examining his cracked and bruised hands. Sage waited for him to go on. "Sometimes my mind kicks into reverse. I'm not crazy," he said. "Well, not *crazy,* crazy. But something creeps up on me. Like a black cloud moves in and takes over. I'm pushing through it. It feels like swimming in murky water. Do you ever get that?"

"No."

Alex went on. "It was like the old swimming hole idea—where we all went in the summer to be in our own hideaway—our own place. We'd be away from the world. Escape from its orders. Those 'what you're supposed to be' kind of rules. But we'd get there…"

"We'd get where?"

"…and the water would be murky instead of clear. There was no way you could see through it. We joked that hell was underneath."

Sage nodded. "And then?"

"We never thought about outgrowing it or what was ahead. Kids don't do that, you know? But as we got older, letting go to jump into murky water got to be downright scary."

Sage stood still, waiting for him to go on.

"Today, the old swimming hole is an alien place. Hard to believe it was the best excitement we could imagine. These days, it's like a symbol for other things. Like toting a gun in some hell hole instead of splashing in a murky swimming hole. To you, it might bring a good childhood vibe. Not to me. Hell, no."

Sage waited, startled that something was coming out. Even so, its scrambled image didn't make much sense.

He went on. "Instead, conjure up blackness, hell, death, damnation, and the worst horror you could imagine. Okay?" He looked at her, and she nodded. "Try putting it in today's context. Then toss in frantic grannies, old men with their teeth on the way out. And kids. It's their ultimate adventure. They think this is some kind of exciting ride. But why are their parents acting so weird?"

Sage sat quietly.

"They're rushing from the shore, crawling or throwing themselves over the sides of the already overloaded boat. Despite their exhaustion, they're scrambling into the worn-out, flimsy, piece-of-shit boat—the bobbing part of a flotilla from Hades." He seemed one breath away from screaming.

"Wait! You're rambling. Slow down."

"—but wait, no. It's not part of anything. All alone. We're all alone! With no one. And no boats nearby in case this voyage all goes to shit." He tried to take a deep breath but instead gasped for air. "Aren't there other boats to help? Nope. And where's the captain? There isn't one! Did he forget to jump in the boat? Wasn't he supposed to guide us? He took our money—our precious coins—all we had! It's not just a bumpy sea that makes us queasy. The giant waves toss the boat upward, then drop it back onto roaring water. We're being tossed and dropped. The sun is like fire. And the old woman. The great wave took her with it. The sun is like fire. And the old woman struggles to pull herself into the boat, but she's weak and clinging to the side. No one is helping her! She'll drown without help. An enormous wave slaps over the boat, pulling her into the sea."

Sage sat, transfixed. Alex momentarily returned to the present, took a long breath, then went on.

"This isn't what they had in mind. Sure, they thought it would be tough, but this? They're thrown from side to side, raised up and slammed down to their seats… but what? You said seats? No one has seats! And they're headed into those vicious, blasting waves. Most left their lives behind and came with all they had. That was pretty much nothing. Nope, this ain't no carnival ride, folks." He dragged his hands over his face and through his hair. "Even those who fished for their livelihood weren't prepared. Hell, were they thinking of their ancestors' fishing boats? Maybe, but they weren't crammed to the gills with a crowd of people. And sure, they'd met unforgiving storms in the Aegean. But this? Did they think they were pushing off on an adventure? Who thought they were headed to death? I'll bet no one."

There was another, even longer pause. "Sorry. You still with me?" Alex looked up as if he'd just awakened.

"Yup." She struggled to set aside her own dream. "I was thinking of something similar, putting my thoughts into the vision along with yours. Do you do that?"

"Not if I can help it." He took another breath, which seemed to Sage almost like a gasp.

"Then how do you steady your head?"

"Obviously not well." He gave a half-hearted grin.

"Huh. You need to find your way past that."

"I've been told. Doesn't seem to work in the midst of remembering chaos. Flashbacks don't allow that kind of peaceful reflection." He looked down at his wrist. "Let's get going. Time's a wastin'."

* * *

Sage stepped back from her bedroom window. The sky was a heavy gray. For those watching TV news, it was a signal the fire was still active. Had to be. Even with her summers in the West and research in far-flung places, she'd had no experience with fire. Her best bet would be latching on to Alex while she had the chance.

She'd awakened once during the night and pondered that thought. Sometimes, her best ideas came around 3:00 a.m. Forming a chain of logical steps seemed easier. Trying to recapture them at dawn was a whole other task. Even if she scribbled them on the pad by her bed or dictated them to her phone, they mostly seemed ill-conceived in the light of day. Sometimes, they seemed downright crazy.

Falling asleep seemed futile. Sage hoped that wasn't the case as far as throwing her fate in with Alex. Did it seem rational? Or would she feel compelled to follow his every order? The very idea unnerved her, and she exhaled a moan that startled her in its anger and despair.

* * *

Alex scrambled from his cabin door, crossed the sagging porch with two long strides, and then launched himself down the steps. "Hurry. Get up here. Did anyone see you?"

Sage shrugged her shoulders. "Pretty sure not. But if they did, I look like I was walking after a long run. I checked up and down the road, before I dodged over. And I left Fabio behind for now."

Alex looked beyond her, then half dragged, half elbowed, her through the door. "Your bravery is back after a day of rest? Or is your quirky brain intrigued by the underhanded stuff?"

"Nope. Not entirely. But I won't let those creeps get me or my sanity. I guess that means I'm either stupid or maybe just mad as hell. But the idea of trying to grab land—the all-out wrong of it—that just infuriates me."

"Shhh." Alex put a finger to his lips and dipped his head toward the bedroom. A young boy peered from around the doorway. Sage guessed he could be around six or seven years old. "Qadri, this is our friend Sage," Alex said slowly. "She's come to visit us."

Sage smiled and gave a small wave. "Hi, Qadri. It's very nice to meet you." She turned to Alex. "He doesn't know English?"

"Back in Afghanistan, we figured the less English he knew, the safer. We did our best to keep him away from it."

"And who takes care of him when you're out?"

"Jax, my partner. We're both teaching him English," Alex said. "He's learning bits and pieces. It amazes me, and we try to talk a lot. He's a real trooper. I hope he's going to stay here. Came back with me from Afghanistan. We've temporarily lost track of his parents," Alex whispered. "That is, I hope it's only temporary. His father worked with us on the sly, so we need to get him out. Looks like he missed a couple early flights. They were pretty loaded, and it wouldn't be unlike him to let someone else on first—and of course, he's not the type who would hang onto the landing gear." He smiled at Qadri, "Jax will be coming to hang out with you, be with you," he said slowly and clearly. "We'll wait with you until he comes." He turned to Sage. "There are a couple trustworthy people willing to keep an eye on him in a pinch, but I

43

avoid it any way I can. It's a hard juggling act when I need to keep my work quiet. I can trust the pastor over at the church because I've talked to him privately. He shouldn't be one to let the cat out of the bag, so to speak. I didn't have a choice."

"Qadri, can you and Jax hang out for a while? He'll probably bring some work with him." The boy nodded and grinned.

Alex turned back to the window. "Okay. Let's hear your plan—you've got one, right? You're a scientist, but we're going to cast a spell?"

"Why not? I'm multi-talented. And I'm glad you're fairly calm. Otherwise, I'd be worried—like I was when you went off into space for me yesterday." Sage waited for him to respond.

"It comes and goes. I'm a hell of a lot better than I used to be. But get this. I'm into this because of my job. I can't just bail or buckle."

"There's no alternative, is there?" Sage noted. "And I'm already caught in it. Besides, they could wreck my property, and it's my home. I want my life back, and I'll fight for that. Like I said—I'm in. You're stuck with me."

"Great. Same goes the other way."

"Okay, then. Just stop scowling."

* * *

The back door at Loonatic's rattled as Sage pushed inside, arms laden with assorted junk mail and books. Fabio stood at attention, taking in the smell of food. The disheveled kitchen showed signs of a hectic but profitable lunch hour.

"Hey, my stomach was growling at the post office, and I realized I'd missed lunch. But I guess I'm too late?" She could still catch the aroma of a hot grill.

"Officially, yes. But you've got special privileges. And the recycling bag is out back." Crystal grinned as she turned from the mammoth range. "Oh my God! What happened to you?"

Sage leaned against the freezer and sighed. "We need to talk," she whispered. "And we need a quiet place to do it. Is anyone else around?"

"Not right here. The place is quiet—just a couple coffee dawdlers way in the rear of the dining room." In a far corner, two hikers lingered over a map, their packs resting on a worn Oriental rug. Soothing jazz clarinet lulled in the background. Pete Fountain? Perhaps, given Crystal's Southern sensibilities.

"I can help prep dinner salads if that helps."

"No. Sit. And you too, Fabio. Oh, and MT's out back getting things ready for tonight's dinner. With a husband disappearing, it's good to keep her busy." Crystal's sigh was somewhere between pity and that of a mother whose child needed special attention. "Oh, and there's some lake trout gumbo left."

Sage nodded and flopped into her friend's rolling desk chair. The cushion had a wayward poking spring, but no matter. It was really the armrests she sought. She scooted sideways, away from a stack of recipes and notes for the next week's menu.

Crystal brought a steaming mug and spoon, then stopped and leaned across the metal prep table, still wearing her intense frown. "Hope that's not too salty. It's getting toward the bottom of the pot. I can add more broth."

Sage sipped. "It's fine. Perfect. Best medicine I could have." Slouching back, she launched into a replay of the last few days: the night attack and Alex appearing from nowhere the next morning. How it was hard to get a fix on him, even if he did give good first aid. She summarized, then announced, "What happened to me might relate to Colin's disappearance—or even to that bizarre chat with Holton." She closed her eyes and took a deep breath. "Here the story gets messy."

"You're saying it hasn't already?"

Sage shrugged. "I'm not sure what to do."

Crystal finally smiled. "Sounds like you're asking for my opinion. Right?"

"Look. There's even more strange stuff going on around here. Not just with Colin." Sage lowered her voice. "I need to be able to tell you this. And we can't share it with anyone."

Crystal's frown returned. "Is this a life and death issue?"

"It may be." Sage's spoon clinked in the bottom of the mug, and she engaged her best pleading tone. "Got any more of this?" She pulled her body forward from the chair before Crystal could speak.

"Sit. Stay." Fabio's head popped up, and he looked toward Crystal with obvious confusion. "Not you. Your mom."

Crystal returned with a full mug, and Sage blew to cool the soup before going on. She told Alex she'd be poking around. How he demanded she stay out of his way. And how the discussion somehow triggered Alex to blow his cop cover. "Seriously, I don't know how I did it—how I managed to box him into a corner. I don't think he was in top form. He seemed to be on edge. Then, suddenly, he drifted off into something like a dream state. And not a pleasant one."

Crystal shook her head, trying to regroup. "Sure it's not just his personality?"

"I don't think so. What I saw is clearly not good—especially since he's some kind of government cop. And working on some kind of crucial investigation."

"Here?" Crystal squeaked. "Do we know exactly what he's investigating?"

Sage shook her head. "Not entirely. But we know the who part."

"And that would be…"

"Holton Denys."

"Yikes. His boss."

"So-called boss. Point is, I'm going to be around here until we know something. Then the question becomes, was I an idiot to elbow in and try to team up with him?"

"I don't suppose I get much time to process this?" Crystal rested her fists against her chin and glowered at the tablecloth.

"Well, hey… what are the options? You're my friend. Tell me. Should I have thrown up my hands and run? But where things stand now, that seems impossible. I think somehow I—or something else—turned a corner."

"Yeah, I'm your friend. And you know I'm a sissy. If it didn't look like there was at least a hint that your dad wasn't somehow involved in this, I'd say run for dear life. But I think you're not going to do that."

"Me? You think I'm suddenly some brave Amazon? Not likely. But you're right. We don't know how much this affects Colin, but it seems odd they wouldn't somehow be related. You know what I mean? I'm kind of listening to my gut here."

"And besides that, look who just rescued you from certain death."

"Oh, come on. I would have climbed out of that gulley."

"Then what?" Crystal shook her head. "You'd go off poking around on your own? I know you. You might as well have some backup."

"Yeah, but this guy seems a little deranged. Like I said, how sane is a guy who slips up like he did?"

"Right. He may be deranged, but he's determined." Crystal grinned. "I mean, the way things have been going, I think we need a little levity. And if you're going to stick your neck out at all, you might as well have some help. But where your dad is concerned, it could be more than your neck."

"Get serious. I'm thinking we need to clearly consider the pros and cons here. As far as trying to keep this quiet, I don't know how I could avoid telling you with all that's going on. But I swear he didn't mean for the cat to be out of the bag. I mean, I don't think he meant to trip over himself. Maybe he's more together than I think. We just have to make sure we're tight-lipped. Can we do that with three of us involved instead of just two?"

"Okay. I agree it appears Alex can provide some level of protection—in spite of being a little screwed up. You said he has a partner, right? If that's the case, I think you're better off tossing your hat in the ring rather than going it alone. Whoever is behind this probably knows you won't be backing off. And without some kind of protection, you could be in deep weeds. Do I sound like I'm trying to talk you into it? Frankly, I'm not sure how you could have gotten in this deep." Crystal's voice slid up an octave. "And in what? Two or three days? It's crazy enough that I do think your choices are limited. Yup, I guess I'd rather see you with some kind of shield."

"What? You don't think my voodoo shield is enough?"

Crystal frowned.

"Hey, that was a joke. Give me a little credit. You said we're looking for levity."

"Okay, I think we've hammered it out. Alex is edgy about secrecy. How much do you want me to know?"

"I think it's good if you're in the loop to some extent, just so you can raise the flag if there's trouble we can't get out of. We're going to have to play it by ear. Wow, I can't believe I'm talking like this."

"Hey, girl, have I ever let you down before? I say we're in this together." They licked their thumbs and pressed them together.

"Mission agreed," Sage said. "But by the way. What's the story about the thumbs? We've been doing it for quite a while. You're the only person I know who does that."

"I'm not sure. We always did that in high school. It's kind of like sealing the deal. Or saying good luck. It's for special friends—like a pact."

"Okay, then give me something to help you here," Sage said. "I still need to relax, and you also gave me a free lunch."

"I can't turn that down," Crystal said. "Help me finish clearing tables." She tossed a used placemat toward a skewed stack two tables away. "And besides, look who's here—Montana!" She gestured toward an alcove where an older woman sat, carefully folding dinner napkins.

Sage darted toward her friend. "Never guessed I'd find you here! Is this a regular thing?" MT's tall, wiry frame hunched over the table. Sage noticed her fingers had become knobby. She looked very much alone, and her hair was grayer than Sage remembered.

"Your friend Crystal thinks I need to keep busy." She looked up at Sage with watery eyes, but her entire face lit into a puckish smile. She reminded Sage of a Scandinavian doll whose head was made from a shriveled apple. "I suppose she told you about Watson."

"She did. I'm so sorry." Sage wrapped her hands around MT's and gave them a gentle but extended squeeze. "She said he'd developed some signs of Alzheimer's. That's a tough thing." Sage knew there was more, and she waited. Better to let MT take the lead.

The older woman shifted in her chair. "Well, yes, that's part of it. Everyone's afraid to talk about it. He actually drove off early this spring. Never came back. Found the old Jeep about fifteen miles away but never found him. We're hoping it gets easier once the leaves come down. Of course, with the fire…" She stared ahead, avoiding Sage's eyes.

Sage rubbed Montana's hand with her own, feeling the thin skin shift easily over the protruding bones. "Are you all right at your place, out there alone?" She spoke softly, wanting to say how sorry she was all over again, but judging she shouldn't. This was one strong woman—in her head anyway, if not her body. At least up to now, all the reports indicated the fire wasn't headed in her direction.

"Oh, yes. But it would be lovely if you'd come out. Take a stroll down memory lane with me." The fierce independence was still there but had softened. "Soon, all right? Day after tomorrow?" She grinned and gave Sage's hand a loving pat. "Make it for lunch. I've got your favorite watermelon pickles."

* * *

Alex sat at the laptop, head in his hands. It was time to simply sit and think. Let the thoughts flow without trying to control them. Just let them tumble out. Hadn't he just had this conversation with himself? And now to have it again? He slammed a fist on the table. His mind trailed back. His thoughts circled. And recircled. They'd talked about this in a group session; guys spread in a circle with their throats in a knot.

He got up for a beer. Strike that thought about her being attractive—or at least interesting. He wasn't sure he could stand being around her. For one thing, he couldn't tolerate flaky omens. If she happened to be a college professor, fine, but how *could* she be when she was such a ditz? He picked up the beer, downing it quickly. He tossed the empty can and went back for a third one. His mind drifted back to his earliest glimpse of her. He'd been out of his mind, for sure. And he reminded himself that looks aren't everything. In fact, she'd suddenly stopped looking good to him. Or looking even mildly interesting. No, she struck him more like a pain in the ass, especially with the weird personality.

Damn beer was warm. She was a handful. He wanted her out, and the sooner, the better. But he was stuck working with her. *With* her? He couldn't get out of it. And it could threaten his own job. Even worse, she knew the lay of the land and the people he needed to work around. Workaround. That's right, he needed a workaround. A way to get her sidelined. But if she knew it, the jig would be up. Damn. It would almost be comical if this weren't such a serious issue. Who told him he was a good people person? Where she was concerned, he clearly was not. He wanted her out. Out. She was not only flaky but potentially dangerous. He had enough trouble battling his own issues without having to worry about her screwing things up. How could she be a scientist and be so... so...

He pounded the desk with his fist. She could put all their lives in jeopardy. He'd been in war zones that were less dangerous. And she had a habit of unpredictability. Yeah, they could get into a tight situation, and she could blow the whole thing. What the hell was he thinking to even get her out of the gully? It was the dog's fault. Should have run him over on the road. No. That wasn't right. Get a grip. He loved animals. Well, he could dream, couldn't he? And this was supposed to be a thinking session. Pondering. Don't push the ideas away. Just go with them.

Jax ringing. Forget the damn phone. He can wait. Need to grab some control. Lay down the law. Sneak off without her. Stop sharing the info. Go visit with that little old lady. MT? That was it.

* * *

Sage turned right off the county road onto MT's long drive. The name on the mailbox caught her eye. Watson Mason. Why would parents give a kid a first name that matched part of his last name? Because both were old family names? Because they found it quirky or simply liked the sound of it? Never mind that through childhood, he loathed being called "Wats 'is name," and then later in life, "*Old* Wats 'is name." But more important, what had happened to him?

MT opened the door before Sage could knock. She'd probably been waiting and watching. "How long since you've been out here for a visit?" The sleeves of her faded flannel shirt hung over her hands, and she stopped talking only long enough to roll them well past her elbows. Next came her habit of brushing a wayward lock of hair from her face. "You been hiding out in Colorado all this time?"

"Mostly. I've got to keep my own research on track at the same time I'm teaching. It gets to be a handful." Sage stared again at MT's flannel shirt, wondering if it was the same one she recalled from childhood. Pale greenish plaid crisscrossed with yellow lines that always reminded her of late summer grasses. Today, the fabric looked softer and thinner than she remembered.

"Well, it's great to have you here, but I'm sorry you had to rush back to check on your dad." She heaved a long sigh and shook her head. "Seems like there's an epidemic of missing in action. Any new ideas?"

Sage swallowed the panic that rose in her. "Not really. Guess I'll just hang around, keep an ear to the ground, and see what's up. I'm trying to sit tight."

"You caught me cleaning. Come on back while I finish the scrubbing."

Sage stared at the unusual square tub in the corner in all its bright green glory. "Remember when Mom and I came to visit? I used to sit in here—without water, mind you—and read Nancy Drew or your *National Geographics*. That's how I got interested in science. Especially archaeology." She wondered how such a quirky bathroom fixture got there.

MT grinned. "And then, if it was winter, I'd build a fire. You loved that." She shook her head and gazed at Sage with a sudden weariness. "You'd ask for the story about how Wats got all those rocks. How he built me that stone fireplace on this spot. Back when we first got the land."

Sage blinked hard and could only nod.

"I used to tell him he'd give Lake Superior a bare shoreline, always making off with two or three. I didn't want my future husband in jail for stealing boulders. He said he was *collecting* them for his sweet Montana." Her giggle sounded like her younger self. "Of course, some came from the property, too."

"And then you built the house…" Sage urged her friend on with the story she'd heard countless times.

"It came together like a jigsaw puzzle. We kept moving around, room by room. We finally had a finished house built around the fireplace."

"And I see you've been cutting wood. That's a decent stack."

MT shrugged. "'Fraid I can't take credit for that. Seems I've made a new friend, and he helped me out. That new guy who's been around lately. Saw him at your friend Crystal's place about a week ago. He was chatting me up while I set tables. Finally, I had to excuse myself because I needed to get back here and split wood."

Sage couldn't help but chuckle. "Alex helped you out, right?" MT had always been a good judge of character, and her opinion would likely be dead on.

"He offered to follow me back and split wood while I told him about the town."

Sage shook her head. So much for common sense. "Geez, MT. You brought a stranger back here? You can't be doing that. But okay, he didn't mug you. What was he like?"

"On the quiet side but good-natured. Not threatening." She seemed eager to have Sage get that part. "Wondered how to get to know the people here. Anyway, that's what he said. I think there was more to it than that. And like I said, he ended up splitting wood."

"Huh. Have to say, it doesn't sound like a bad deal. I know it's a job you're not crazy about."

"Well, when you live out here, you'd better learn to get along. And besides, without Wats around, it gives me something to do." She put an arm around Sage and gave her a gentle squeeze along with a wink. "And I prefer not to freeze my tootsies at night."

Sure, Alex wanted to know the community. If she didn't already sense more, Sage would find it odd that a guy who worked for Holten Denys would pitch in with the work.

Apparently, MT had similar thoughts. "The way he trained those puppy brown eyes on me—or were they blue? I could see the wheels turning. I'm willing to say there was something else going on with him." She blew out a long breath. "Hank said he was hanging around the outfitters, too. Seems he wants to know the workings of this place. But if he's on the side of the enemy, it sure doesn't seem like it."

Sage felt some unease but also still relief, along with a twinge of excitement. Yet she couldn't let on what she knew. "True. Something doesn't fit. People actually like him. Even my dog likes him."

"Do you think he's some kind of cop?" Sometimes MT's intuition was uncanny. "It's almost like his questions were in one place, but his mind was in another. I've had talks with cops before. And those CO guys—the conservation officers. They're direct. Matter of fact. But with this guy, his brain was in two places."

MT whacked her palm against the side of her head. "It's confusing. I'm not sure what to think. He's not what he claims to be, girl. There's something else going on with him. He's got—what do you say? More than one agenda? Mark my words." She shook a bony finger at Sage. "Oh, and he wanted to know about building plans for that resort complex. Like he was trying to figure out how much we all knew about it. Strange, don't you think?"

"But did you feel like you trusted him?"

"Bottom line? Probably. Yes. All I'm saying is, just watch him. There's a lot more there than meets the eye."

* * *

"Okay. You found Judd cleaning up the studio when you got home." Alex kicked back in Colin's chair, rested his feet on the desk and drummed his fingers on the armrests. "I'd think a studio like this would be dusty and dirty all the time. Why clean in such a frenzy?"

"Absolutely. It must have been driving my father crazy. He used to say we work with dirt—and that we'd be casting it all over the place." Sage leaned up from the desk, rolled her chair back and brushed off her elbows. "See what I mean?"

"I'd say the current situation puts a new light on things." Alex tossed a rounded piece of granite between his hands while he pondered. "You've known Judd all your life. Would he be good at making a complex plan? Or would he most likely just up and grab Colin? And we don't have a 'why,' do we?"

"Go on. That's how brainstorming works."

"Look. The key is whether we're sure your father is really missing. Setting up an accident or some kind of trap would mean there'd be cops all over the place trying to find a body. Instead, Judd leaves open the possibility that Colin has merely taken off." Alex paused to think. "And at the same time, maybe he drives around in Colin's car and wearing Colin's hat. No one else around here wears a fedora, so the silhouette of that in the car—along with sunglasses and a pipe—could be a decent deception."

"What? You didn't mention that."

"Sorry. Forgot. The idea is to set up sightings of Colin or make it look like he's been here. That makes it easier to arrange—and manipulate—a timeline, right? And the result is that we don't know when he actually disappeared."

"But that's so much work on Judd's part. Way too complex."

Alex began to pace. "Sure. But we both know something's up. His car's here, but the canoe is gone. Are we supposed to just up and assume he went off and had an accident—or maybe somebody's planned accident? If that were the case, there'd be search parties scouring the land from here to Canada, right?"

"Right. But my father's gotten more careful in his later years. He lets people know where he's going. It's tempting—and hopeful—to think he might have gone off somewhere, but I don't think that's the case. My gut tells me this was well thought out. Probably by someone other than Colin."

"Okay. I hate to put it this way. If your father met with foul play, he may be nearer than we think." He watched for a reaction from Sage, knowing his words were clear. "We need to consider all the odds."

"I know." Sage took a long breath. "We should start with the studio. We spent a lot of time together there. If he's trying to send some kind of message, I'd say that's where it would be."

* * *

Sage moved a wobbly step ladder to a side wall, then edged a hand along a high storage shelf that ran its length. A collection of corrugated boxes stashed with endless newspaper clippings shared space with three-ring binders, empty cans and broken tools. She took another step on the ladder, then groaned with frustration. A layer of choking dust made breathing difficult.

"Wait. I see something. Looks like an old five-by-seven envelope. Maybe the manila kind. It's bent in half and jammed in a tight space. Like where the ceiling joist meets the rafter."

She tried to shift her weight with no luck. "I can't pull it out. We need something like a pocket knife to scrape away a sliver of the beam. That way, I should be able to wiggle it out. I don't know how old it is, so we don't want to tear it or mess up any label." She held back her hand slowly, hoping not to cough or sneeze while on the wobbly ladder. "Whew. Sure is dusty. But that's a pottery studio for you. Too bad it's soaked up some moisture along the roof line—but I guess that's no surprise either."

She rested against the ladder and tried to wave the dust away. "There's a chunk of river rock for a paperweight. You wouldn't see it from down below unless you looked pretty hard."

"You think your father really expected you to find that? Hey, don't lean so much!" Alex yelled. "Last thing I want is to scrape you off the floor."

"Hey. Relax. Judd turned this place upside down," she said, "so I'm not sure if he found the message box I was telling you about. It still turns up every year or so with a message from Colin—like when I get home from my summer teaching. He'd always leave some kind of sign around when I was a kid. It meant there was a message in the box, and I'd have to find it. Sometimes, he'd leave a clue about where to find the chimes. Or once in a while, the destination was a particular place in nature he wanted me to see—like maybe a new nest or a beaver dam in progress. A couple times, the note said, 'Don't get your mother riled.'" Sage stifled a laugh over the idea. "There were times when Colin used me as a go-between to test the water. Was that manipulative? Probably. But I didn't mind. Sometimes, just the idea of getting my parents to communicate—even with me as a broker—was okay."

"Keep going and watch your head," Alex coaxed. "You're coming to a corner with one of those triangular shelves."

Sage scanned the next series of wooden beams before dragging the ladder to a new position. "Where's that damn box? Britta may have spotted it. It has a lock on it, and it takes one of those tiny keys that came with old diaries."

"Like you couldn't just rip a shoe box apart without a key?"

"Hey, play along here. I was a kid. It was pretend, for God's sake. Geez, I hope Judd didn't carry it out and toss it. He's never been one for sentiment." She tested the ladder again for balance and then climbed to the next step. It took several attempts to stretch back to the widest shelves before she felt cardboard wedged between supplies and the rafter. "Bingo! I think I've got it. This isn't one of the usual spots. It's been moved, but at least it's here."

She grasped the old cardboard with its collage of red foil hearts and paper doilies and waved it at Alex. "See what a crafty kid I was in second grade? I think I showed my father's inclination toward creativity, don't you?" She turned the box over. "Looks like something was slid under the lid without using the key."

"So, do you have one? I know you won't want to chance messing up the box."

"Of course. Stuck in Silly Putty under the second desk drawer on the left."

Sage shook the box. "It sounds like a piece of paper bouncing around in there."

"Well, open it!" He passed her the key, and she read. *You found the purple pin! Brava! Writing on your sister's BD—sure hope you find this.*

"Huh. It's pretty long."

"When's your sister's birthday?"

"She's a Cancer."

"When—is—it?"

"June 30th."

Hope this finds you well.

"For crying out loud, Colin, get on with it."

In a mess—not sure how deep. If something happens to me, need you to take action.

"That's him all right. Take action." Sage drew a long breath and read on.

Stumbled on poss illegal activity re new resort. Talked abt wanting our land. Maybe more than that. Money laund? No addl details------ safer if you don't know. If worst happens, go to state authorities, not locals. Do NOT tell anyone else. Keep this note. BTW, Judd has issues. Keep dist and don't ask Qs.

Sage sighed. "Does he mean without somehow tipping off Judd?"

"I'd say that's his point, yes."

Lots more to this. Be careful—so sorry.

Lv you—Dad

"He hid that message *here*?" Alex was nearly ballistic. "That's completely insane. What were the chances you'd find it? And when did he find the time to go through this idiotic routine? Is everything a game to you people? He could be killed... or you... or any of us if we stumbled in the wrong direction. You all belong in padded cells for your own safety!"

Sage handed over the note. "Try to say calm, okay? It's hard to figure out if Judd is involved with something illegal or if he's just got a twisted mind and problems of his own." She slid the box back and moved the ladder across the room. "No sense advertising our search."

"Right, but take the box with you. Let's not make things easier for him." Alex struggled to reclaim his patience. "We already know he's been counterfeiting Colin's work—we just don't know why or how much. And this note hints at something way beyond making knockoffs. You sure your father wouldn't have inadvertently stumbled on other scams related to art? Or maybe on something way beyond the art world? There's news about weird international coverups all the time."

"You mean like online? Colin? No way." Sage shook her head. "He wouldn't waste time on the internet if his life depended on it.

Wrong word. Sorry. And why does everything have to be international? Don't you think that's a bit of a stretch? Well?"

"Here's what strikes me. Think about it. You two are of the same mind. Take the note you found. He knew you'd go looking for some kind of message. Assuming your father came up with a way to reach you—and warn you—it's likely he'd be telling you there's way more going on than pottery. I'm guessing your dad is saying Judd has his fingers in something else—not just clay."

"That's my father. He'd figure no one would know where to look—or, for that matter, even be looking. I guess Colin was pretty sure he could depend on me. But up in the rafters? Seriously? That's less than one chance in a million—but then I guess we've always been on the same wavelength."

"Sure it's weird," Alex admitted. "But I also remind myself that you're all a little off. And that box was like what? Kind of an idol, right? Your dad knew you'd be poking around in the studio." He paused, then went on. "He'd know you'd get the sense something was wrong. You two have one hell of a vibe going on. Sure, Judd's been around for years, but he'd never pick up on it."

"Right. Now what?

* * *

Below a lakeside rest stop, Alex stood on wet sand and panned his field glasses along the far shoreline. He wasn't sure what he would see, and in truth, he hoped to see nothing unusual. The rock cliffs around him were monumental and treacherous. Then, balancing on a large boulder, he scanned north and south. He'd never experienced miles of shoreline rock that massive. A bristling sensation like static electricity ran through his body.

He followed a path back to the parking area and studied the view around him. Was that where Sage had pointed earlier when they faced inland? She'd mentioned a convenient series of wide, natural steps in the rocks nearby. Right now, he had little interest in geological wonders. But the area around the steps might serve as a vantage point for someone watching Sage's property. Turning right, he saw a small drive near Crystal's restaurant. It probably led to the parking area for Lunatics. Off the path, a long but clear trail led toward a series of cabins. For anyone watching activity in that stretch, it provided a good view, especially with the network of trails and near the clear-cut to the east.

Alex watched smoke rising from a burn, but he had no idea how far away it was. Luckily, fire data was updated hourly. He wondered how early loggers, settlers or trappers could judge the distance of such an inferno—especially without GPS. His gut said the current portion of the fire hadn't been a natural occurrence. But was that just his usual paranoia? Accidental fires cropped up now and then from careless canoeists or lightning strikes. Was this a warning? Or an outright threat to those determined to maintain thousands of acres of national forest?

He gave a long whistle as he backed away from the shoreline as if to punctuate his frustration, anger, and amazement at how his objectives had gotten away from him. And yes, even a bit of wonder at how things might evolve over the next few days. There was no way to plan. He could only wait.

As Alex turned back toward the shore, another image overtook him: Lesvos. The trip of 176 nautical miles from Santorini to help. He had failed. Lost his edge. People weren't saved. Instead, they died. He heard screaming and pleas for help. His feet were leaden, and his mind had stopped working. Go, go, go! He was running toward the water, arms outstretched. A woman was screaming. He couldn't understand her, but somehow, he knew she was screaming for the rest of her family. She kept trying to go back into the water, and he held her back. She fought. Clawed at him. Punched him as she tried to break away. They found her husband drowned and washed ashore. She bent over him, sobbing and repeating his name, and Alex could see she also held a small stuffed animal. So there was a child. Children?

What would it be like to go back? What purpose would it serve? Could he be rid of the horrible flashbacks? It was like PTSD. It probably *was* PTSD. But thought he could handle it. But he wasn't. There were daily angry outbursts, and the noise in his head seemed to come from nowhere. Of course, the noise itself wasn't apparent to anyone else, but it drowned out his consciousness, his perception. It wracked his soul. No one would get it.

The faces and the voices were the worst. If he had the power to tune out and go forward, that would help. And then afterward, he'd need to decompress. He'd read about the aftereffects of such a shock, still not wanting to believe they related to himself. It was as if one side of his brain told him he was weak, and the other insisted that, as a human being, he was responding naturally and compassionately. He needed to accept that. Maybe with acceptance, he'd get to the mindset he needed—where he could provide the help without inflicting insanity on himself. He'd known guys like Corey Lindquist, the macho dude from Dakota—also a couple women—who still struggled with violent events, yet he didn't want to put himself in that place. Some got over it; others didn't. Some who didn't became victims themselves, not just of the mental anguish, but of suicide. There was the tough-as-nails, muscular guy who flung himself off a bridge. Alex knew a move like that wasn't helping anyone, and he was still sure his own demons would never get in the way. He continued to wonder if a trip back might help. He turned out the bed light, picked up his cell and hit the oldies app. A little Elvis was good for the soul. He closed his eyes, hoping the night would be silent and peaceful. He had his decision. It was made; that was it. Forward toward sanity. A tough time ahead, but he could handle it.

* * *

Alex was unusually quiet. Sage took the wheel and spoke to break the silence. "When you first came here, you probably took the expressway from Duluth to Two Harbors."

"Yup."

"This time, I'm giving you a lakeside tour." She turned onto a narrow, paved road close to Lake Superior. "Back in the day, this was the only route up the shore. Just shy of thirty miles, then on through Two Harbors. Bet you haven't been up that far, right?"

"Seriously? With all the other crap going on?"

She ignored him. "Back around the late eighteen hundreds, the railroad went up to the iron range to load ore," she said. "That's northeast of us. Anyhow, today, the old railroad is a draw for tourists."

"Ever think about getting a mike and telling folks all the stories?"

Sage went on. "And right now, we're headed through woods and open areas, never too far from the lake.

"For me, it's like another world," she said. "Thing is, the speed limit's too high. You've got to watch for deer—especially the little guys following their mothers across the road. Can't tell you how many times I've had idiots blast their horns at me for going too slow."

The landscape had changed little over the years, and in this case, it bore the familiar look of a dry summer landscape with faded colors that seemed not quite real, more like an overexposed photo. As they drove toward Duluth, cabins dotted the rocky shoreline, and the tan dust drifting above side roads blended with smoke into a lingering haze. Sage recalled picking blueberries with her mother on a rocky slope and tramping with her father over lava flows that were millions of years old. Today, she felt old herself.

She ignored Alex's scowl and pointed out small resorts, homes and cabins that seemed to clutch the rocky shorelines and cafes set back from the water. She praised a landmark smoked fish shop in the small town of Knife River and slowed on curves that offered closer views of the lake.

"I'm going to pull off so you can see."

There was no reaction from Alex. She went on, talking about the 1960s and 1970s when small fish called smelt were still abundant. At the end of every April, fishermen—including Colin—clogged the emptying, netting tubs and garbage cans of the silvery fish to freeze for winter.

Years later, gradual erosion along the cliffs and banks had destroyed more than one of Sage's favorite overlooks. In some cases, complete portions of cliffs—including their original lookouts—had crumbled down the high slopes to the water. Reinforced concrete replaced the old stone barriers. The former charm was gone, but if one focused on the endless view of water, the view remained staggering.

At last, Alex spoke. "Was this supposed to be a peaceful drive or a lecture?"

"You're here, and you might as well get a taste of our history—and the lay of the land. And who's to know how long you'll stay, right? Maybe longer than you think."

* * *

C. L. Matsch gallery had it all. Occupying a stately stone mansion near the eastern outskirts of Duluth, it bore the name of a beloved local art collector. The gallery featured work by a range of regional artists, both newcomers and others who were widely known. Colin's work had a far-reaching reputation. The upcoming fete would include not only his latest pieces but a broad view of his life's work.

Sage was surprised by Alex's interest in the upcoming exhibit, which would officially open at week's end. "Isn't this amazing?" He stepped closer to a large photo. "Look at how those yellow and gold colors jump out—they look like some kind of soft neon—how does she do that?"

"There's kind of an other-worldly look, isn't there?" Sage crept closer, focused a few inches away, then stepped back. "I have no clue. It might be the artist's secret," she said.

"Sage, how lovely to see you." Hector, the gallery owner, moved toward her with outstretched arms. A group of onlookers turned their ears in his direction. "We weren't expecting you so soon."

Seems like no one was, Sage thought. "The lighter walls look fabulous."

"Yes, well, we wanted to create a blank canvas for the art itself, if you will."

"Of course," Sage nodded.

He turned to Alex. "Stop by on opening night, and I bet the photographer would explain the process she used in that photo," he said. "Artists like to know their work excites patrons. In fact, I'm guessing she has a couple more like this hidden away. You should put your dibs on one early."

Alex gave a short nod, and Hector next turned to Sage. "I wanted to get you away from the action." He pointed toward the unpacking area and spoke in nearly a whisper. "We heard your father took off somewhere. Is there any news?" The remark caught Sage off guard. She turned her head slowly. "No." How did he know Colin was missing? For the moment, she chose not to ask.

"I trust you'll let me know when you hear something." Hector's voice was nearly a whisper. "Given my long association with your father—and, of course, you—you know my concern." They returned to the main gallery. "I hope you'll be able to stop by and meet some of the dignitaries."

"Dignitaries? In Duluth?" Sage's eyes opened wide. "I know you expect arts columnists from regional papers, but dignitaries? Really?" She picked up a pair of hammered silver earrings. "I'm glad you expanded to showing jewelry this time. We have some pretty phenomenal artists around these parts."

"Well, my dear, you've got me there—or should I say here?" He chuckled. "I was hoping for some curators and directors from the five-state area. Typically, they're not very prompt with their replies. Another would normally come, but he's now out West. Uppity, but then I wouldn't know. He probably sees a lot of cowboy art these days." He raised his eyebrows before going on. "Too narrow for me as far as subject matter. We're not sure he'll pop in. He's a little more highly placed. Or should I say we're a little below his gaze?" Hector paused momentarily, and Sage waited. "In any case, we anticipate a quiet opening."

Despite the manager's uncertainty, the gallery was being fully prepped for the event of the season. "If your father is tied up elsewhere and can't be here, we're hoping you could review his individual pieces and approve our presentation."

Sage felt a slight pang at Hector's choice of words.

"We'll have his pieces displayed with those of regional landscape artists. We want to do well by everyone who is showing their work. I'm thinking we'll put the silver jewelry near the front—see those glass cases? It'll be easier to keep an eye on small items that way."

Sage grinned. "I see what you mean about putting the jewelry up there. I've already gone and nearly walked off with a pair of hammered earrings."

"I knew you had theft in your personality," Hector laughed. "Oh, and so I don't forget, I expect you saw the letter I sent to your father?"

Sage turned and looked at Hector. "No. I just returned from Colorado. But my concern has been about who would actually deliver the pieces. I wanted to make sure they got to you. Too much other stuff going on."

"Actually, I just got into town myself. Sorry for the confusion. I was looking, and it turns out they were here all along."

"Did Colin bring them?"

"Oh, no. No," Hector said. "It was his assistant who brought them a couple days ago. He said you were back, and we needed to start combing for other items. We discussed that a couple months ago. I thought Colin had already determined what he was sending. Let me check my notes."

"Alex, look at this," Sage whispered as she turned a large bowl over and over in her hands.

"I know. His work is incredible. Even as a person with no talent, I can see that."

"Not what I mean. This isn't my father's work. This is a knockoff. A fake. The—that's the little stamp on the bottom—is oh so faint. It looks exactly like my dad's, but it's light and kind of hard to make out. See? It's like a little calling card with a logo. And see how the proportion of the foot—the rim on the bottom—is different on this one?"

"I don't get it. The only person who'd have access would be..."

"Judd. But to what purpose?" Sage continued, "If Colin weren't around, Judd wouldn't benefit from any sales here anyway."

"Maybe he wants us to think Colin was working more recently than he really was. What if your father really disappeared earlier? Wait. That might fit with our theory of the fake Colin people have spotted driving around. And why he never stopped to chat. He'd just wave to folks and just keep going. It's like a plot concocted by a rookie. Or else by someone who is completely deranged."

"That's really the way to put it. I'm sure I—and probably plenty of other folks—have fallen for Judd's schemes for years," Sage said. "It breaks my heart to think of all the people he's managed to dupe."

"He must have been hell on wheels in elementary school. Didn't they have special rooms for those guys? Like with bars—or at least hand cuffs?"

"Oh yeah, I know. Sometimes, you have to wonder if those jerks are even aware of what they're up to. I think Judd is. My God, his poor mother. You could tell she adored him."

"I guess there's one lesson we need to keep in mind. Never trust that guy. One way or another, the result could be dangerous."

* * *

Sage slipped through the back door at Lunatics. The man at the bar had his back to her, so she ducked into the coat room for a better view. Reddish hair. Scruffy. Mostly attractive. She crept up behind him. "I'm guessing you're Jackson, right?"

The man started, yet kept his head down and gazed into his beer glass. "Who wants to know?"

"Very funny. This place is a small point on the map. Alex mentioned you, and there's no one else around who fits the bill." Sage turned her best scowl on him. "In fact, I can see how you two must be friends."

"That's how your logic works?"

"Don't get cute with me," she said and yelled toward the backroom for a Fitger's pale.

He straightened in his chair and finally turned to face her. "I was told you have an attitude."

"Well, now you know." She stared at him dead on. "Glad you're upfront about it."

"Okay. You win. I'm low on brain power right now. What do you want? It's Saturday, and I haven't recovered from last night. And by the way, you can call me Jax."

Sage snagged a bar chair, reached for her beer and took a slow sip. "Ah…still the best. So, what's up with Alex?"

Jax shook his head. "You get right to it, don't you?" He stretched for a napkin, hoisted the back of his jeans and wiped a beer ring off the bar. "Okay. He suffers from a tough career."

"Go on."

"He worked in the Middle East. Afghanistan. One of those jobs that don't really exist. You get what I'm saying? From what I gather, things didn't go well for him. He doesn't talk about it. I learned everything from his buddies. He was young in terms of how he approached things... always trying to push the boundaries."

He looked at Sage to be sure she was tracking with him. "Worked with a family whose son was an interpreter. They also had a very young child. The plan was to eventually get the whole family out of the country. The kid wanted to go to college in the US, and it was a dangerous situation, particularly because if you hang with the US, your family can be in danger."

"I'm not liking the sound of this."

"You asked for it. As I heard the story, the kid spent a lot of time with Alex. Can't say what Alex's personality was like then, but he probably was looser than he is now."

"Right. I think he's kind of uptight." Then she stopped and pondered. "But still... it strikes me that his way of working is on the creative side—if you get what I mean. I think he could still bend the rules plenty."

"Maybe, but a lot of his outlook comes from his combat experience. Trying not to make mistakes. Apparently, the kid was killed because he hung out too much with Alex. Word was he adored him like a big brother. A sniper picked him off, and the family was torn apart. Alex always felt he hadn't been enough of a protector. People like Alex tend to take responsibility even if they don't play much part in the outcome. Turns out the sniper had it in for the family anyway, so it was kind of the Middle Eastern version of the Hatfields and McCoys."

"Huh. So, it was a revenge killing for something between the families?"

"Yeah, or the tribes. I'm not sure. Like I said, I'm not that up on the whole deal, but you get my drift. He can't let go of it. And realize I'm not telling you this firsthand. I might have blurred some of the details."

"Got it."

Jax stretched his neck, tapped his fingers on the bar and went on. "Sure, his unit would always try to protect the kid, and there are a lot of interpreters in those kinds of situations. But it's not always as easy as those guys would like. So what if you've got a gun. You can't be responsible for every idiot around you who is insane with some passion or another."

It seemed like a no-win situation. "Do those guys get any kind of counseling?"

"Some. Probably nowhere near enough. It sticks with you, you know? Especially when you've lost someone who idolized you and someone you thought you could look out for—even though you both were clearly in a huge danger zone constantly."

"Then what? He came back here?"

Jax took a long draw on his beer. "Yeah, trying to transition back to a normal life. His tendency to break the rules—or ignore them completely—didn't fit real well in a structured group."

Sage sighed and shook her head. "Where's the balance between pushing the boundaries and staying within the law? Sounds like a bungled TV script."

"He's kind of negotiated his own way of operating. He goes under the radar. Being a well-regarded hotshot with superior skills, he pretty much gets to make his own calls. Within reason, of course. It probably works best that way."

"That's how he'd know where to be and what to do? Or not to do?"

"Right. There's a field branch that keeps track of him in a loose way, but he's mostly a lone wolf. On dubious cases, I get to tag along as backup. That's as long as I don't interfere too much. Other times, I'm forced to get him back on track."

"How much of a yarn are you really spinning for me? I mean, doesn't his kind of work—plotting calculated moves, knowing who your enemies are, constantly watching your back—demand at least some minimal kind of structure? Some focus on the rules?"

"Oh, that's pretty true all the way around. Course, you have to realize that when a guy like Alex is idolized like he is, we all tend to go for the best side of the story."

Sage scowled and waited for Jax to go on.

"Just kidding. But it's all true. My interpretation of how he's gotta give up some of the blame is true, too. Not sure how that's going to happen. There's a lot below the surface with him, and it's hard to drag that out. I wish he'd go back; maybe try to see things from a different perspective."

"Sure, Jax, but a child died pretty much under his watch. That leaves parents with unstoppable rage. It goes along with the sorrow. You think the family would accept anything he said?" Sage pushed her empty glass aside. "Thanks for the info. But I sense there's a lot more to all of this. And right now, I'm thinking you might be the only one with a clear head."

"That's doubtful, but I can use the atta boy." Jax shrugged his shoulders. "And I'll cover the beer."

* * *

Oh, Dad, where are you? From her position in the bow, Sage looked to her left and scanned the nearby shore. She tried to avoid looking to the right at the seemingly endless expanse of Lake Superior. Just as it could take down an ore boat in a hellish storm, it could easily swamp a canoe—even on this seemingly windless day and in one of the small bays. While Superior had always seemed beautiful, Sage reminded herself that its spirit could also be demonic. During her infrequent summer visits, she watched the water glimmer and sparkle, just as she had when she was a child.

But this summer was different. She wondered if it was her imagination. The water itself seemed darker than its usual grayish blue. Its sparkle was gone, and it offered only an indescribable eeriness. Maybe her mood was responsible. But no, the darkness she felt came from a more unsettling source.

Alex broke into her thoughts. "You sure you're up to this?"

"No, but I want to look for myself, and it's something I wouldn't do alone."

"And that's why you're taking me along?"

"You got it."

"You sure know how to flatter a guy. By the way, I was thinking. Where is your mother now?"

"She died."

"I'm sorry. Your father really left chaos in his wake, didn't he?"

"Totally."

"And your sister?"

"She's great, really—coming here for part of the summer. Maybe longer. She lives in Ann Arbor and just finished grad school. Now she's thinking about totally shifting gears—wants a freer life like mine. By the way, that's a joke." Sage stopped paddling for a moment as if to ponder.

"Hey. Snap out of it," Alex said. "I'm trying to turn us, and you're fighting me."

"Sorry. I need to tell her my life is not all that free—at least not in the academic world. Right now, she'll be testing what it's like to be an artist, working in Colin's studio. But then, all that could change by next week."

"Are you two close?"

"Sort of, surprisingly. You wouldn't think so. But I guess we both have sympathy for each other."

"How's that?"

"Resolving our big problem of how to get together," Sage said. "With our current lives, it's hard to work out schedules. But if I quit teaching, that could change. Last we talked, she thought she might spend part of the summer here. Depending on what she plans to do, she could use part of the studio," Sage paused and laughed. "That ought to rattle Judd's cage."

Alex raised a brow. "You mean he's territorial or just crazy? But wait. I think it could be both, right? Anyway, I didn't know you taught."

"I don't advertise it. Right now, I think of myself as in transition. It's a first-class case of burnout. I've got a leave of absence for this fall, so that gives me time to think."

From seemingly nowhere, a wave pitched the canoe sideways, and with it, Sage's thoughts. Colin's outer office and the dust of the inner studio flashed through her mind. But wait. An essential object was either missing or out of place. Strange the vision hadn't struck while she poked around the studio rafters. Or when she'd first arrived and played a mental rerun of her father and daughter memories. Had Colin moved their secret mailbox? In her mind's eye, Sage couldn't recall seeing it in the room, at least not in any of its usual places. She tried to envision the decorated shoebox in the open cupboards near the maps.

Another rogue wave, this time from a fishing boat, slid toward them. "Hey, did you fall asleep up there? Paddle! I didn't bring my scuba gear!" Alex turned his paddle to head them closer to shore. "Where's your head?"

"Just going through his office again in my mind, thinking how it's different from before. How some things seem out of place—or missing." She closed her eyes for a moment as if to bring a clearer picture to mind. "There was a box—just an old Cuban cigar box—that I decorated as a kid. It had a heart-shaped paper doily on it and red foil for Valentine's Day. Colin and I used to leave notes to each other in it, but the other person had to find it first. I wonder where it is—and if he left anything in it now."

"That's a huge stretch, don't you think?"

"Not necessarily. We knew each other's minds. If my father wanted to communicate with me and not let anyone know, there's a slim possibility. Especially with the weird stuff going on now. We need to look." She took a long breath. "Knowing Colin, I'm thinking he left more than one box. Kind of like backup."

* * *

"Can you imagine getting tar balls on your butt?"

"Uh, no." Here's another weird conversation starter, Alex thought.

"You know, from sitting on a beach? I ruined some of my best field clothes that way—assuming field clothes are good clothes, that is."

"Is this so-called discussion going anywhere?"

"Well, picture the Mediterranean," she said. "Think of a romantic interlude on the shore. Soft breezes, a kind of filmy light, a hint of salty air… the call to prayer from the tower? Then you decide everything around you is so otherworldly that you'll just sit through the sunset and soak up the night. You don't need some kind of spirit friend. It's all in front of you."

Sage's vision—or her imaginings—seemed disconnected but sincere. Still, Alex tried again. "There's a point here?"

"Just listen. Maybe you hang around all night and stand up at sunrise. Or maybe you've just been out for an afternoon. Some of life's incredible experiences are short ones. Anyway, you eventually get up, and your butt is full of tar balls. So..." but before she could continue, he cut her off.

"Please. Don't torture me like this. Do you have a point?"

"Stop interrupting me."

"That wasn't an interruption," Alex said. "It was a plea for help. And stop snarling, would you?"

"Okay. Well..." She closed her eyes and sat back for a moment, then took a quick breath. "I think it's that you should always look for more than one message that you're going to get from a place—or from an experience in general."

Alex sighed, and Sage went on. "What if you let that idea lead you back to where we were a couple days ago? Yeah, we've got the turquoise sky, the sand that's been heating up for us, the air that's part mist—but more salt that you can actually taste on your skin—and those black blobs. Our life has black blobs—so can we figure out what they're telegraphing in spite of the big picture? And every picture's different. Like off California, tar might mean there's oil seeping right out of the earth. Whereas, in the Mediterranean—let's say from North Africa or the Middle East—tar balls tend to come from pipeline leaks near shore or from along all those oil transport lanes." She exhaled in frustration. "Some things in life can be incredibly bad, yet maybe they go along with some very valuable experiences. Like... not all tar balls are the same."

"Sheesh. And the big picture would be what? Something like 'into every life some tar must stick?' Nothing you just said makes sense."

"Could be, but I'm also saying there are different ways to interpret what we see. Like that idyllic scene at Judd's place."

"What? Idyllic? No way! It was borderline creepy. And I come from battlefields."

"Exactly. Beneath the surface, it wasn't an idyllic place at all. Is there anything that lurks in your memory? That taunts you? That literally pokes you between the eyes, begging for your attention? I'm thinking of something not so much related to Judd or Colin, but something more... well... maybe more like a message in the form of a sign. Like..."

"Stop, will you? I'm not tracking with you at all."

Sage took a slow, deep breath to control her frustration. "When we were kids, Judd and I spent days making up games about hanging out in the forest—as its guests. What if the woods were more... sociable... welcoming? Do you think that could help us find Colin?" She paused and raised her arms, pleading. "Quit rolling your eyes."

"Well, far be it from me to say, but allow me to ask the woods to cut you some slack—because you're a nutcase." Alex looked down, took a deep breath and shook his head.

"Like you couldn't pinpoint anything strange when we were driving back and forth?" Sage paused, hoping to prod Alex's memory. "Nothing you sensed felt remotely off? Not a single thing begging you to look closer?"

"Not so. I'm trained to look for things or events that strike me as being out of place." He stood up, brushed off sand and dried leaves, then made exaggerated motions to observe the seat of his pants.

"Now what?" Sage scowled.

"Just making sure I didn't miss any tar balls."

* * *

"You've been implying Judd is kind of scattered," Sage said. "Like in the midst of all this, his mind is really elsewhere?"

"Not necessarily. Or maybe sort of. More like it's scattered in more places at once. Could be. Not all criminals strive for the perfect crime. They can't. Many of them simply aren't capable of planning every detail." Alex paused to clear his head, and he noticed Sage seemed confused as well. "Well, okay. Here's a sample. That little stamp..."

"*The* stamp."

"Right," Alex said. "Not all criminals strive for the perfect crime. They can't—or simply won't be bothered. And lots of those dudes aren't capable of planning the heist itself, let alone every minute detail. Or they figure perfection is too bothersome. Maybe they just lose track of where their plan was headed. I've seen that a lot."

Sage wondered if Alex himself knew where his plan—or thoughts—were headed. "Okay, so?"

"This seems kind of convoluted, but look. We're checking out Judd's house. We find a 'Colin knockoff' stamp, presumably made by Judd, to use on his fakes. But Judd still makes his own pottery, and we know he's got his own little 'Judd' stamp too. Are you with me?"

"Sure," Sage said. "That's partly the point. It's one of those things with side benefits. If you can steal a real one, that's great."

On the other hand," Alex said, "it's possible this part of Judd's plan is just a ploy to disguise what's really going on. You know. A misdirection. Or a distraction. Maybe it's a sleight-of-hand trick to focus your attention away from the real action. And just wait. If that's what's up, I'd say it's going to become apparent before too long."

"Naw. That's a great idea, but the Judd I know isn't that clever." Sage moved closer to her father's work table. "And look. Here's one of Colin's real stamps. His cartouche. Like the one Judd made." She held it for Alex to inspect. "There's the 'C' for Colin and then the tiny spruce tree next to it. I bet he circled back and made another one so Colin wouldn't know one of his own was missing." Turning to take in the whole view, Sage thought hard about the best approach. "What else do you want to see? Where should we start?"

"With Judd going in and out— then activity like supply deliveries or just plain sweeping—no one thought about keeping this place undisturbed. He's been hauling stuff back and forth, and who knows what's intentionally been misplaced. Oh, yeah. You can bet he thought of that while he was messing around in here."

Alex nodded. "That's one problem with keeping law enforcement out of this for now. If we were playing this by the book, the whole area would be cordoned off."

Sage closed her eyes and stood motionless at Colin's desk. "Wait. The purple pin."

Alex leaned in closer, hands on his hips. "Can you be a little more expansive?"

"I pulled it from the map. And... I recall holding it." She clapped her hands against the pocket of her jeans as if to find something that might be misplaced.

"If it's so important, where is it now?"

"That part doesn't matter. Probably in the dirty laundry. What matters is where it was on the map."

Alex leveled his eyes at her and droned in a slow monotone. "So. Where... was... it... on... the... map?"

"It went like this," Sage explained. "The red and blue pins were for Colin's favorite portages and lookouts. The purple one was a signal to me."

"Slow down, will you?" Alex griped. "This is the most half-assed, slipshod, unprofessional and bogus investigation I've ever been part of." He took a long breath as if to clear his head. "But never mind. What's with the purple?"

"Okay. Think you've covered everything? If it makes you feel better, let's not call it an investigation. How about an informal chat? Sometimes, we do science that way, too. Can you just cool your jets?" Sage clamped her jaw, and the next words were nearly a hiss. "You handle the part with Holton Denys, and I'll focus on Colin. We know there's a remote possibility the two are related, right?"

"So far, I'm not seeing that." He stepped forward to get a closer look at the map, then looked over his shoulder with an impatient head shake.

"Ah, but you've agreed to help me."

"I don't think so—when was that? No, I'm just tagging along with this farce. And hoping if we find something you won't have managed to make it inadmissible."

"I'm a scientist. I think ahead," Sage snapped. "And you're sounding pretty pompous. Look, I just asked for one afternoon, okay?"

"Oh, so now it's not that woo-woo thing? Now we're actually

based in some kind of thought process?" His voice had a snarl that seemed more annoyed than before. "All right. What I'm saying is, this whole thing sounds a little far-fetched. Unless this is really how you and your dad communicated." He took a quick breath. "Okay? So communicate."

"Yes, listen. More than that. It's really how we interacted. How we spent time together and how he taught me things. A pin in the map was a signal. It was like 'let the games begin.'" She poked the map with an index finger for emphasis. "There should be a bunch of points scattered around that don't match portages or his favorite hiking spots. Those would be from the purple pins." Her voice rose with excitement. "If an empty pinhole doesn't match up with something Colin and I did earlier, there's a chance it could mean something now." She looked at Alex for confirmation. "The pin is probably still in my pocket, but I'll bet I can find a hole in the map. In fact, I plan to cover every inch until I do."

"Did you think that through or get it from a spirit?" Alex smirked in spite of his frustration.

"Of course, I thought it through."

The map was an overwhelming patchwork. Small maps with larger type were taped to the sides of the large main map. The smaller maps and those of a different scale sometimes overlapped each other lengthwise or side to side. The result was a jumbled patchwork for anyone not familiar with the area. In several areas, Colin had placed maps with different distance scales and colors directly over the larger map. On the ten-foot length of wall, the result was dizzying.

"And I suspect you plan to cover every inch."

"That's partly how I learned to find my way around as a kid. We were out hiking once, and Dad gave me an old Brunton compass. Then he told me it was time I learned how to find my way home."

"I hope he didn't leave you there?"

"Of course not. But see? Look at this spot. You can tell the purple pin was here once. It's at the top of that crest. He wouldn't be dragging a canoe up there to portage. We had lunch up there once to check on how far we could see." She ran her hand over the map.

"Lightly! You don't want to flatten the pinprick!" Alex rocked back and forth on his toes.

"Lightly? You lighten up! I'm the one who suggested this, so you know damn well I'm working carefully. I have very sensitive fingers." She stepped back to wiggle them near his face.

"Great. Right. Now, can you focus on where you were standing when you took the last pin out?"

Sage leaned back from the map. "There's part of the trail that goes north of MT's place. Rough terrain up there. Used to be an old logging road. There was a way to get back there on foot, and Mom used to hike with me for blueberries. Dad liked the solitude."

"Good. Lead on," Alex said. He pointed at the old Brunton compass he'd seen earlier on her shelf. This time, it rested on her belt.

"I know it's ancient and worn on the outside," she said. "But still, it's backup when I want to be out following a map." She turned to her map and its wavy topographic lines. "They kept me from getting lost many a time."

"Okay, Ms. Crockett, where's the place that's close to the purple pin? The one on the big wall. Let's try to locate ourselves in that area."

"We want to check out the lay of the land," Sage said. "Colin used the pin to show roughly where we were. First, look around the areas that have some elevation, just not too steep. They'd have to be ones a little girl could get to."

They worked the lower areas first, hoping something important would be easy to spot.

Alex seemed intrigued by Sage's approach. "Can you remember where you were standing or what you were looking at?"

"Maybe I could see more from a different angle. Can you give me a boost?"

"Remember," Alex said. "We didn't bring a first aid kit."

"Take it easy. I've done this a million times. I can eliminate some of the map's pinholes. Sometimes, it's easy to connect them with other places we've been to or from nearby overlooks. This one's from a couple summers ago when I was home for a month. Like old times." Fabio dropped to the ground, rolled on his side and gave a sigh Sage interpreted as boredom. "I know—you remember this spot, don't you, buddy? It was quite a trek."

"Colin sure has a probing mind," Alex said. "Does that come from his artistic side?"

"That's why I'm guessing he's done it again now." She scanned the map and immediately discounted a half dozen pinholes. "Here." She pointed to what looked like an older hole. "And see? By that creek bed? I think we had a picnic there. Looks like you might have pulled over some flatter stones to sit on. All these years... kind of like our own family archaeology." She moved farther to the left. "Here's one I don't recall—bet I had dirty fingers again. And then the one across from the letter F—see? Right where you're moving your hand. And another one. I'd say we have three mystery holes."

"Too bad your dad couldn't have made this easier. Like maybe making the new hole—if there is one—a bigger size," He shook his head in frustration.

"I know. And I agree. But Colin was hooked on those colored plastic push pins. The kind that come with maps. I'm sorry, but this is what we've got to work with."

"Hell. I'm beginning to wonder if your father really wants to be found," Alex fumed. "You get that this is totally insane, right? You're thinking we're supposed to believe his captors—or whatever—chose one of these so-called newer spots because the map is cleaner there? Plus, his life might be in danger, and he's refused to stop fooling around and wasting time. If and when we manage to find him, I hope he has a good explanation." He was surprised that Sage seemed to hold her ground.

"You finished? We need to look for holes that seem newer—with less smudging around them."

"What'll it take to check them?"

"We can get fairly close by car, and then it's a pretty easy hike to these two." She tapped the map. "The third is a little farther, but there's another old trail that takes us fairly close. The trek won't be bad at all."

"Okay. Let's do it. C'mon, Fabio. Time's a wastin'."

* * *

After futile probing—and for exactly what, they weren't certain, Sage and Alex trudged back to the Jeep.

"I've been patient with your approach," Alex said. "And we'll keep looking. But hell. I think we can assume this whole disappearing thing wasn't a quick fishing trip." He paused for a moment. "Unless it was, I'll take care of putting out the word—and I'll do it quietly. We'll keep it to ourselves. This one's definitely not going to be the scene for having a rescue happen. But I figured seeing the lay of the land would be useful. In short, I've done this before, and we need a new approach…"

Sage broke in. "Sounds more like you're giving up. And I want Crystal to know what's going on, too."

"Not really. Not giving up. But I've given your idea a chance," Alex said. "Really. I wanted to be accommodating, but this is enough. It's going to be about four hours of poking around—including the drive. We're clearly losing precious time."

There was no reply from Sage.

"Sure, I'd like to see your plan happen," Alex said. "But it's time-consuming and not very realistic. You've said Colin loved playing father-and-daughter games. But right now we're well beyond common sense. It would help to know what we're looking for. Think we'll find more here? The last two pinholes were a washout."

"If it makes you feel better, I don't recall being here before with Colin. Sure, I've hiked this spot, but I can't tie it to any purple pins."

They fought underbrush up a small slope, then looked out over the landscape. "This GPS app is the greatest. How'd you know it would work out here?"

"Reception around here keeps getting better—and it sure beats carrying a dirty topo map that's been folded and refolded a dozen times. But like I said—I always carry backup options." She patted the small pack on her hip.

"Hey, Fabio, stick around." Alex watched the dog trot off purposefully. Sometimes, he bounced playfully through the underbrush. Chipmunks? Now and again, he stopped, raised his head and stood like a frozen statue. The next minute, he was zooming in circles and figure eights. "Fabio, you sensing some kind of animal, or you been smoking something?" Alex yelled.

"It's okay. He won't go far. And who knows what he'll find. Could be some kind of animal that's freaked out by sensing fire."

The air was sometimes still, while at other times, a filmy breeze rippled lightly through the leaves. "It's weird not to hear birds. And I'm surprised the smoke isn't stronger. Mind you, I'm not complaining."

"Listen!" A faint tinkling noise startled Sage. It was hardly discernable and almost otherworldly.

"I don't hear anything," Alex whispered. "What?" he mouthed, standing statue still.

"Sssshh. Listen again." Fabio whined. His head moved as if he was tracking the sound. "Wait for the next breeze. There. Now. Do you hear it?"

"Not sure. Just barely—or maybe it's my imagination. Power of suggestion, you know?" Alex paused and waited. "That faint tinkling... right? The chimes?"

"You got it," Sage said. "We're getting closer. I like to think Colin's trying to show us something. I just can't get a fix on where. If we had just a little more wind, it would be a snap. See what I mean?" There was another slight tinkling, then total silence once again. "Can't believe I'm asking for wind when we've got a fire nipping our heels."

"Let's walk around and see if anything jumps out," Alex suggested. "We can come back pronto or else get a crew out here. Would be easier if we could tell them more."

"Right. I'm marking the map."

The sun was lower in the sky, and the breeze began to fade, leaving them no closer to the chimes. Fabio trotted from the underbrush, and they headed for the car. The trek seemed longer because their legs ached, and the search had failed.

"You do realize your dad is a total nut case, don't you? Who'd go through all this trouble—or effort—to lead us here. It makes no sense. None. And meanwhile, the clock is ticking."

"That's my father for you."

"Okay. I guess you've got me hooked. Or at least I'll cut you some slack. I can admit—well, up to a point—that this strangeness fits what you've told me about him. Plus, he clearly thinks—or hopes?—you're going to follow his trail, so to speak. Or maybe in the beginning, he didn't think this would end up quite so dire."

"We did find something. We just don't know what."

* * *

At the end of the dock, Alex relaxed by skipping stones over the smooth water. Sage sat on her towel as youthful memories passed by—floating in inner tubes, listening to water slap the old rowboat, watching the sun creep closer to the horizon. Despite the restful scene, an eerie foreboding settled over her. It was something dark and treacherous. Could sifting through memories joggle the mind? Somehow, she wasn't sure. She did how her father's base was always his desk.

"To entertain us, he'd hide the chimes in toppled trees or even the studio rafters. Sometimes, he used his old hook to hoist our chimes high into the trees," she said. "When I was young, he retrieved those chimes for me, but only as long as he knew I'd spotted them and pointed." Sage smiled as she remembered. "As I got older, he'd put them farther away."

She heard the faint tinkle of wind chimes on the breeze—but this time, she knew it was her imagination, buzzing with mental and emotional weariness. Again. Then nothing. Were they indeed real? She couldn't detect a clear direction, and the random nature of their melody eerily came to life, then faded. They could be anywhere, choosing to ride the current of wind just to mesmerize her. A rustling of menace settled around her, and she carried a sense of desperation back to the studio.

Once settled in Colin's chair, total exhaustion took over. She leaned back to her favorite position, legs resting atop his desk. When she spoke with Alex, a cloud of frustration remained. "When I first got here," she said, "it didn't strike me right away that the chimes were missing. I mean, they weren't in their usual place by his desk. But they were the least of my worries. All I could think of was 'where could *he* be?""

She tried to recall where everything might have been when Colin started moving it around. "He always put his tools away, but the hook had definitely been out. It was behind his desk, as if to say, look, this is where the chimes usually are, but I've hidden them. And here is the hook, just so you don't miss that fact."

Alex frowned. "Go back. What kind of hints? Like specific messages?"

"Sometimes, he'd just hide them around the property. Or, as I got older, he'd put them farther from the studio. Maybe by the lake... or the gravel pit. Once, he found a way to hang them from under part of the dock—the higher end that's above the water level. That had me fooled for quite a while. Sometimes, he'd leave mysterious clues for me to use in my search. If there's a clue this time, I guess I'm missing it."

"If what you say is typical, he may have come under some kind of duress. Maybe he didn't have time or wasn't able to give you a heads up." Alex searched her face. "Can you try to make an educated guess? Or even take a shot in the dark about what he might have done?"

Sage held her head between her hands and rested her elbows on her knees. "I'm not getting any clues," she said.

"Don't wait for one of those metaphysical moments of yours. Just try putting your mind to it," Alex urged. "Try going back to some of the other times. You're saying this was a pretty frequent game. Does anything stand out? Is there a particular time back then that could give us an idea of where to start today?"

"Well, maybe. Now that you mention it, our old collie found them more than once before I did. I used to think his sixth sense was better than mine. And I think he sometimes heard them when I couldn't."

"That doesn't sound so odd for a dog," Alex said. "Can you give it a try? Assuming your dad didn't hide them someplace in Duluth, could you stake out a territory to check? Even if you or Fabio don't come up with anything, maybe the search itself will rattle your memory." He went on. "We know very roughly how far away today's hiding place is. We need to take Fabio back with us. I'm guessing he'll be able to close in again."

"This is awfully basic—elementary, isn't it?"

"Yes, but that's what your father wanted, I think. No one but the two of you knew about the chimes. I'm betting he 'reverse-engineered' his instructions or clues so they might appear insignificant—even childish—and be ignored by anyone other than you. Think about it. You've developed an ear for volume and distance. If someone else hears chimes, they'll either think they're losing their mind or that it's a sound carried from elsewhere. Maybe someone's idea of a soothing atmosphere at a campsite."

"Right. The ruse was good enough that we missed it the first time, too. But we heard the chimes—and pinned them down—so that has to be it."

Fabio edged closer, sidled up and gazed at Alex with what looked like a sly grin. As an afterthought, he gave a loud belch.

"Geez, you smell like dead fish," Alex said. "What did you eat out there?"

Fabio hung his head. For a moment, there was silence, then the sound of retching. "Oh, crap," Alex moaned. "He's starting to barf."

Up came a mass of green grass and several bits of broken twigs. There also was a small, cream-colored stone with a silvery indentation. The other end of the piece had two longish protrusions.

"Uh-oh. Sage, you need to get over here with paper towels—or whatever it is you use for disgusting messes. I'm not touching this."

Still, the worn chunk was intriguing enough that he poked it with his pen. "Whoaaa. What have we here?" Fabio whined while Alex stared in amazement. "You got a pair of tweezers? I think we have a tooth."

Sage turned the odd grayish fragment over in her hand. "It's not Colin's. See that hole? Looks like there was a filling once, but Colin had—has—perfect teeth."

"Huh. Bet I could make an educated, but maybe far out, guess." Alex took a long breath and raised an eyebrow.

"You think maybe it belongs to MT's husband? Watson?"

"I'm wondering if we just found a thread that ties our efforts together." He turned the specimen over and over, studying it with Sage's pocket loupe.

"And that's what the wind chimes were meant to signal? Good boy!" She grinned down at Fabio. "You're a better investigator than your friend Alex here. But seriously, trying to link this with the chimes—or the other way around—it's way too big a stretch. Given what Colin would do, it's just plain overkill."

"Bad choice of words," Alex said. "But just for the hell of it, Fabio. I don't suppose you can tell us where you found this. Right?"

"I'll bet he can come pretty close. Are you ready to play archaeologist?" Sage asked.

"You mean me or Fabio?"

Sage didn't answer, but her mind was racing. "Anyway, can you have Jax round up a crew? But not anyone from town—word travels, you know."

"Oh, yeah. Just ask, and that guy can do anything."

"Great. Meanwhile, I'll hustle down to Duluth," she said. "I'm hoping I can snag a sifting screen on campus. If it works for archaeology, it'll work for sleuthing. I had no idea I'd need one, and of course, I didn't want to short the Colorado group." She paused to consider what else should be done. "I'll help with the setup so everything looks real. We'll go from there. It's got to be a quiet operation—and if there's a question, we'll call it a summer session project. Or some kind of site survey. Learning a new technique. We'll figure it out. Anyhow, you're in charge. It shouldn't take long to identify the tooth, and some old X-rays might back up the experiment. I bet MT's dentist would jump at some undercover sleuthing—especially for Wats, his longtime friend. A phone request from MT was enough to pique his interest. He also like the idea of being 'a dentist with a closed mouth.'"

"I'm going to take it to MT." Alex seemed determined.

"But I should go along."

"Nope, I think this will be just between MT and me," he said. "She'll need you to check in later."

"But doesn't it need to go to a police lab first? Isn't there some kind of documented procedure? You keep doing things that seem like they'd lead to inadmissible." Sage crossed her arms.

"How often do you think I stand on procedure? Most times, I need to work fast. I rarely care what *has* to be done. I just know what I'm going to do right now. In this case, MT is not your typical faint-hearted woman."

"Wait a minute! Whoooaạaa. You think *I'm* a typical faint-hearted woman?" Sage glowered and took a step toward Alex. "I watch bison butting heads and killing each other,

"You know what I mean. MT has quite a bit of character stuffed into that little body. She's a bundle of courage and feistiness. It might do her good to get the news this way."

"Well, that's a stretch. But she has kind of taken to you. Still, this whole mess goes more rogue by the minute."

* * *

The long driveway to MT's house was rutty from the last downpour. Alex bumped cautiously around the potholes, cursing the grit and mud collecting on his undercarriage. Good thing he didn't have a flashy car that was low to the ground.

MT met him. "Alex, it's good you've come. And I trust you." She swept a strand of unruly hair off her face. "I've done my crying over the last couple months. It's best to finally know he's not with us—even if we may never know why."

That was MT—practical. Not one to surrender to events that would weaken her. Alex knew she grieved, but also how strong she was. Still, recent months showed her mind had begun to wander. Bills sometimes remained in her mailbox. Bed sheets hung on the clothesline in the midst of rain.

"MT, you're tough as nails. Or rocks. You can let down, you know." He stretched out his hand to show her the tooth. She nodded quietly. That was enough. He didn't need to know more.

"Already did that. Oh, yes. Many a night, or sometimes out of the blue in the day. But I couldn't risk getting pulled under. How many times in my years have I said 'that's life'? Well, it is." She looked at Alex with brown, watery eyes.

"Anyway, there's a lot here to keep up on," she said, "so I try to put my thoughts on that." Her mind seemed to wander a bit. "My mother was from Montana. They liked the name, so they gave it to me. And then, the MT part came along later. Wats used to say it had something to do with the post office." She gave a short chuckle and straightened her shoulders. "Anyhow, it's tough to know those bastards are probably close by. I plan to be around when you finally corral them."

* * *

"How did it go?" Sage leaned her elbows on the bar and coddled her beer.

"She one hundred percent identified it. Old Wats had pretty distinctive fillings, apparently. And she must have been plenty used to scrutinizing his teeth."

"How's she doing?"

"Hanging in there." Alex shrugged his shoulders. "Could probably use a visit from you tomorrow."

"Definitely."

"And now we know one part of the puzzle. Hell, when Fabio coughed up that baby, I could have sworn it was going to be your dad's."

"Yeah, I'm not sure what to think. What's your theory?"

"Just a guess, but maybe Wats stumbled onto something he shouldn't have, then started poking around where his nose didn't belong. Our four-footed buddy came across the first clue. Leave it to Fabio. So I expect Wats didn't get too far and didn't get lost driving around. I'm crossing that one off my list," Alex said. "He may have been elderly, but he knew this area like the back of his hand. So, as far as getting lost, that one's off my list. But—and this is crucial—we've got to get a clear idea of when he took off. Sounds like right now he's being classified as a missing person."

"And…"

"Okay, he starts messing where he doesn't belong, and someone offs him. That in itself presents a problem—like they've got to dispose of the body and do it quickly. So, we need to touch base with Jax. And where do we stand with getting that crew in? We need to get going on that grid and go through everything out there. I was hoping to hold off for a while—and

I'm going to forget what we've found for a couple days. I told MT, and she's fine with it. Mostly, she's happy to know he's been found—or that part of him has. The resolution will surely help here, but it's still a lot to cope with. I sense she's pretty tough, and she's gonna need that. I'm sure that will eventually lead to some small bit of resolution. At least she can absorb all this and have some idea of how things went. Then, have some kind of resolution—and I'm not sure what it can be. When this is over, let's hope she can view him as a kind of hero."

* * *

"Stop!"

"You said that before. This is where it's got to stop. Sage bolted from her stool, which toppled to the floor. "Is this the way you try to atone for your so-called past mistakes? The ones you think were your personal responsibility?" She waited for a response, but there wasn't one. "Like the way you remember refugees stuck on sinking boats?"

Alex gripped the edge of the bar, his knuckles whitening. "No!" Then, in one swipe, glasses flew toward the floor.

"Cripe. What's that about? Feeling a need to blow off some steam?" Sage asked. "Thank God you're not a real cop, or you'd lock yourself up." The room became quiet while Alex drew another breath. Sage went on. "Even I know your methods are shaky. Weren't you ever taught to play nice with others?"

"The hell with that!"

"Hey, cool your jets, will you? Whoever connected you to this Holton project is insane. And now we're off on the Wats trail. Have you ever considered following the book? Or is that too mundane for you? You've got to play by at least some kind of rules. Do the rest of your so-called cop buddies…"

"Okay. Stop right now," Alex bellowed.

"No! You listen! Sure, you've got sharp folks hanging in with you. But somehow, they're off in the background while you're out here—crossing the line on your own." Sage struggled to catch her breath. "And where the hell is Jax? You can't just decide to play the enforcer, then end up going rogue."

"Who says so? And by the way, I think an enforcer is someone who's already gone rogue. I know what I'm after. I'm guessing we're at a point where things are going to get touchy pretty quickly. So let's keep our heads on straight and see what happens next."

* * *

Alex was useless. Sage fought to keep her voice even. "So, you're saying Wats saw more than he should, and someone had to get rid of him? I guess if you were running some kind of scam, you wouldn't want a talkative old guy around—especially if he seemed to have some kind of dementia. Who knows what story he could put together?"

"An interesting point. We do know Wats was faking the dementia—or at least most of it." Alex took a deep breath as if to settle himself. "Wish I'd known him. Apparently, he was quite the actor."

"Don't change the subject. Just remember I've noted some of your methods stink."

"Okay. I know. I get it. I'm willing to rethink."

"Seriously. I'll back off and admit it's probably not the best idea to get a crew of archaeologists out to map and sift. That wouldn't be the best plan."

"Not necessarily. I'm not ready to abandon that idea yet," Sage said.

"You never know. Who knows what else is going on with this group of idiots."

"No kidding. When did that thought occur?"

"Look at who's jumping the gun right now." Alex took a deep breath as if trying to unwind. He went on. "I'm a rookie where that's concerned. Okay, I'll give you that. For sure, it has to be done by law enforcement. Unfortunately, there really are limits to the rogue approach, even where I'm concerned."

"Okay, so we sit tight on that." Sage exhaled relief. "What do we do in the meantime?"

"I'd say we all play it by ear and keep things cool around Judd. Has Denys been around to harass you lately?"

"No, at least I don't think so. Hard to know if he was the one that attacked me that night."

"I'm thinking not. He strikes me as the type who wouldn't want to get his hands dirty. If he's involved in any of this, he's got some pretty talented henchmen. On the other hand, so many aspects of this mess seem almost ridiculous."

* * *

The road was dusty, with no sign of tracks, and the house looked deserted. Sage dropped from the pickup and dashed to MT's door.

"MT!"

No answer.

"MT? Are you here?" Alex yelled from across the yard.

Sage ran toward the aging pole barn. Alex heaved aside the corrugated doors as the battered metal groaned. The response from inside was a scraping sound against concrete. It was followed by muffled cursing.

"MT! Are you here? It's Sage!"

A heap of weather-beaten tarp rustled over the floor until it met a stack of rebar propped against a stud. In the midst of crashing metal, MT's irate snarl came from beneath the canvas. "Damn! I'm so mad I could spit tornadoes!"

"MT!" Alex was first to reach the tarp and he flung it aside. Underneath, a bruised and fuming MT gazed up at him. "Judas Priest, I thought you'd never get here. Some damn idiot jumped me. Course, I got a few licks in, too."

Sage felt a sigh of relief. If MT could be cantankerous, she was fine.

Alex was less certain. "Take it easy. Don't rush. Can you stand?" As he helped MT rise to her feet, his eyes scanned the aging building.

The large shed looked like it had just exhaled a deep breath. It was hard to see inside. One part served as a garage for MT's car, and the other housed a rusty John Deere tractor. The other was strewn with relics from Watson's old outfitter business.

"It was the perfect day, you know? I was antsy, and the thought of working outside seemed like good medicine. I mixed copper spray for the early tomatoes over in my little greenhouse, and then I started feeling awful."

"How do you mean? Were you dizzy?"

MT stopped to get her breath. "Not exactly. But something felt bad in my gut. 'Course, I was already out of sorts because my neighbor Eleanor—the one across the field—told me they'd never grow. So it wasn't pain, but a kind of premonition got started. And besides that, with this short growing season, you have to baby them. Tomatoes are always a hope and a prayer up here, you know?"

"Hold up a minute, MT. Go back to that first feeling in your gut."

"I felt like someone was watching. I think I turned in the other direction, and before long, whammy." MT took a long breath. "I think there were two. One kept telling the other to shut up. Do you know what it means to see stars? Next thing I knew, you were calling me, and I was face down under a damn tarp."

"We need to get you checked out. That's a nasty bump," Sage said.

"I don't think they meant anything… permanent. I think they just wanted to scare the bejesus out of me. Well, it didn't work. So they put an egg on my head. Come to think about it, maybe it was just one."

"One egg or one visitor?" Relieved that MT was safe, Alex took a long breath, then hugged her lightly. "Remember," he said, "there were two guys talking." Maybe if she relaxed, the event would be more clear.

Sage realized MT was totally confused. She smiled. "It's good to know we can count on you, MT. Did you see him? Or them?"

"How do you know it was a him?" MT bristled. "Could be that lady realtor was hanging around here."

"Okay, we'll hold out that possibility." Alex raised an eyebrow and looked at Sage. "Tell me what you remember, MT."

"But wait. No. I'm pretty sure it was just one that walloped me. Couldn't see anything because the tarp was over my head pretty quick, and I hit the concrete. A little ice would help, if you don't mind." She paused for a moment and scowled. "Now, but wait. Wait. Somehow I'm thinking there really was one. Yes. Yes. I remember now. Definitely two. One was heading outside to stand watch. Sounded like he tripped over something. He swore a blue streak on the way out, but I didn't know his voice. Anyway, I think he was screaming through his teeth."

Clearly, MT was quite confused. Sage decided patience would be best. "Looks like maybe he stepped on the rake head and whopped himself." She pointed toward one of MT's antiquated rakes near the driveway. "Maybe we need to keep our eyes open around town."

"Always said there's some around here who need their heads examined." MT slapped her overalls and ran her fingers through her hair. She winced as she rolled her shoulders.

"We should have someone take a look at you." Alex picked up MT's crushed sun hat and pressed it back into shape.

"Forget it. I'm fine, so let's get on with it." MT snatched the hat from Alex and carefully set it on her head. "We've got work to do."

* * *

At Loonatic's, they settled into a secluded booth. Although unsettled and fatigued, MT slowly recovered from her attack.

"I guess a shower and a change of clothes are called for," Sage said, "but a cold beer might be better medicine." She noticed MT's hands had stopped shaking.

"Wats always liked this place," MT said. "He got a kick being a thorn in the side of that Denys character. Always tried to figure out what was going on with him. Meanwhile, I was taking notes in the kitchen." She slapped the table and laughed.

"You mean Holton kept trying to figure out Watson? I can't imagine the two of them ever meeting."

"No. No. The other way around." MT shifted on the padded bench as if to settle her mind as well as her body. "Wats would corner him like he was some long-lost relative. Actually, block him into his booth. It happened here more than once. That Denys guy used to claim the back booth, thinking he'd be mostly out of sight but still within earshot. It can get loud in here, you know." She shook her head when the server returned to replenish beers.

"Sometimes, I'd plop down next to Wats. He pretended he was hard of hearing, so he always leaned forward. I played along, taking in as much as I could without pen and paper. Then I'd rush back to the kitchen and scribble notes. The rest of the locals had all they could do to keep straight faces. Wats pretended to chit-chat, and it irked Holton, so he—Wats, I mean—acted feeble and forgetful. He'd try to pump Holton for info, then a few minutes later ask him to repeat it. He figured it was an easy—or maybe safe—way to collect information, even if it took twice as long." She shook her head and cackled. "I had a hard time keeping a straight face." MT reached for a tissue, wiped her eyes, then paused. "Where was I?"

"I think you were going to tell me about Holton's building plans."

"Right. He kept quizzing Wats about who owned what piece of land and about how many acres." She shook her head when a server suggested another beer. "And he was interested in what kind of access it had—road, water or whatever."

"Like he didn't want to go to the county offices or surveyors to figure any of that stuff out?"

MT nodded. "He even asked what the terrain was like and whether many businesses use planes up here."

"How could he not know what the terrain is like? It was baffling to imagine someone posing as a businessperson and not having the slightest idea—or desire—to do what seemed to be necessary research. And then not to document it."

Sage smiled. "This is definitely a new take on operating under the radar." All she wanted to do was find Colin. She tried to appear calm, but her stomach still held a tight knot. There were so many tangled threads, and who knew how many agendas, that her sense of logic was totally jumbled. Should she have become a criminology expert instead of someone who studied ancient cultures? Right now, a freezing storm in Colorado sounded ideal.

"Earth to Sage… earth to Sage," Alex whispered. "Take a break, will you? This entire discussion sounds like a rerun of a long day rather than an effort to move ahead."

"What? You're a cop of sorts. So you should realize this is a review of where we're at. It's not a card club."

"Right." He tried to refocus and pick up on the discussion. "Guess he decided he'd pretty much have to collect his own information—or find someone else—because Wats wasn't being too helpful."

"And this guy doesn't use a computer to check things out?" Sage lifted a brow.

MT went on. "After a while, I suspect Holton decided I was the sharper one and had followed at least part of the questioning." She sat back and shook her head. "So what was he going to do about it? I know he was trying to keep an eye on me—like maybe I was stealing food from the kitchen?" She laughed.

"That man sure tried to keep his cards close to his chest."

"And I kept going back into the kitchen so he'd think I was oblivious—but at the same time, I tried to keep taking notes. I put them on the side of Crystal's fridge with a magnet. You can have them if you want."

"When was this?"

"Well, let's see," MT counted on her fingers. "I guess it would be a week or two before Wats disappeared. So that was something like three weeks ago from now."

"You know, MT, I'm guessing Holton realized you knew more than you let on. I mean, that you were somehow a risk because you understood something, even if Wats didn't. So it could be that was the reason you were attacked. I'll bet things were about to get pretty bad for you. They were out the back door of the garage in no time flat. I'm seriously concerned about you staying out at your place tonight."

"No way." MT huffed. "I wouldn't rest anywhere else. That barking dog alarm you gave me would drive off an army. I've got things covered. I'll call you when I tuck in and again when I'm up at five thirty in the morning."

Sage cringed. "And any time in between, all right? I'm really not on board with your plan. But I sense I can't talk you out of it."

"Damn right." MT smacked the table with her fist. "Besides. They'd be fools to circle back so soon."

* * *

"Not a good plan to keep important info near the fridge," Sage called across the kitchen. Curiosity about MT's notes wasn't enough to keep her from a refrigerator raid.

"What's this brown stuff?" she yelled with her head inside.

"Leave it." Crystal snapped from her place at the range.

"Hey, that's what I say to Fabio when he tries to sneak food behind my back."

"Then I bet you also know the drop-it command?"

Sage pushed the door behind her hard enough to catch Crystal's attention again. "Hey—get back to work. You're the one who said we don't have time to waste."

How true, Sage thought. There were more questions than ever. MT's notes were a jumble of paper scraps, many nearly impossible to decipher, some ripped from the corners of old envelopes, others scribbled on the back of Crystal's shopping lists. A series of Post-it notes occupied their own area, now stuck together in a foot-long stream toward the back of the refrigerator. Sage would have chosen a color less obtrusive than lime green. And although she'd developed her own version of shorthand for writing in field books, Sage struggled to decipher MT's scramble of word fragments, dates and long, meandering arrows. Simply sorting them in order would be a challenge.

* * *

A worn bench at the end of the family dock was perfect for twilight contemplation. Daylight was fading, and smoke had been in the air so long that Sage barely noticed it. She sorted through recent events possibly related to Colin's disappearance. Who was responsible? Maybe someone thought the fire was a convenient time to toss their fate into the mix. What was the chance Judd could be even remotely connected? And she knew even less about the possible role Alex played. Shouldn't there be a definite protocol for finding her father? What else was going on in the background?

* * *

"Good thing Judd's trip to Duluth will take a while," Sage said. "I wouldn't try breaking into his house if he was on a quick jaunt. But who knows what his response would be if he caught us there? Plus, I haven't been inside for ages. Maybe we should have brought helmets in case the roof caves."

"No worries," Alex said. "He'll be stranded in Duluth for a while. Should have sent him along with a sleeping bag." He tried to hold back a laugh. "But here's the good part. I had Jax do a little work on his car—and he's a man of many talents. In fact, he's probably having the time of his life, even if he gets caught at it."

"Really? I'm curious."

"Judd gets down to Duluth with his to-do list. He delivers Colin's work to the gallery on the main drag, then probably parks somewhere off Superior Street."

"You mean, so it's less likely that someone spots him?"

"Right. He goes off to do his other business," Alex explained. "Meanwhile, Jax tinkers around and switches some kind of wire that's tied in with the ignition… I think that's what he said. Well, maybe not exactly. Anyhow, I don't mess with that stuff. So don't ask me. I don't fix."

Sage grinned. "So?"

"This gets better. Unfortunately for Judd, Something's faulty with the new one. Like I said. Don't ask me."

"He'll be at a standstill?"

"Right, and he'll get towed." Alex went on. "Clearly, he won't be pleased—that's saying it mildly. He'll demand that it gets fixed pronto. Says he'll wait. And God forbid, an experienced mechanic's likely to be baffled. I can see it now—Mr. Big Muscled Mechanic knows everything looks fine, but the damn car won't start. They might eventually find the problem—which I suppose will have been the result of so-called pranksters—how do I know?" He gave an evil smile. "I'm no expert. And there's more. Jax figured he could add some kind of tracker. Anyhow, Judd's temporarily stuck. Good plan, right?" Alex stifled a grin. "And I'm guessing he's the kind of guy who's not very big on patience."

* * *

They parked in a small lot at the head of a hiking trail. That way, they could link up with another trail that wound toward Judd's cabin. "Actually, the house is down an old county road, then another half mile on an even older dirt road. We can easily pick it up by cutting across by the fire tower. Sure, we could drive in, but I don't want to leave any tracks."

"This must be hell in winter," Alex said.

"Everything seems like hell in the winter here," Sage told him. "But really, you get used to it, and then it's not so bad. Actually, you learn to love it. But you really should see it in the fall. The leaves turn bright yellow. It's like living in that golden world I told you about."

"How come you know this spot so well?"

"Like I said, Judd and I played here as kids. This is where he lived with his mother, Emily. She died just after Judd finished high school. She was sort of sickly. Mom and I used to visit her, and we'd bring baked bread or a casserole. She was always very shy and never wanted to take from us."

"What about her husband?"

"Word spread that he ran off," Sage said. "She always kept to herself and never wanted to talk about it. It was clearly an embarrassment to her. I guess, in a way, I could understand that. And times were different then. I know she was shy, to begin with, but it got worse. She just seemed to shrink away."

"So, with a kid your age close by, this was kind of a second home?"

"Off and on. Enough so I can still put my fingers on the key—that's if it's still in its old place."

On the outside, the house was more worn than she remembered. One shutter was gone, and several others hung precariously. Peeling paint clung to the siding, exposing dried, gray wood. Nothing a good power washing couldn't help—unless it took off even more paint. The flower beds were overgrown with weeds. There was no sign of the well-tended wild flowers Emily had coaxed each year from spring to fall. An old pump house leaned a few feet back from the path. Its foundation was made from boulders the size of bowling balls picked from surrounding glacial deposits.

There was no sign of the key, but Alex noticed a thin crack of light near the door jamb. "Guess we don't need the key. That wasn't a good place to keep it anyway."

"So you're saying we might as well climb through a window?"

"Not really. Too dangerous, given all the glass. I've got a driver's license and credit card. Normally, they'd work, but they're too thick to get through the door crack. Got anything thinner?"

Sage felt for the zip pocket in her jeans. "Got it. How about a free dessert from Loonatic's?"

"Can't pass on that. You ready for a break-in?"

"You bet. Go for it!"

"Careful." Alex edged past her. "This place looks like a pigsty."

Damp men's clothes covered the floor. Sage wondered what that was about. Broken pottery looked as if it had been smashed into as many pieces as possible. She noticed some of the shards came from her father's work. Others appeared to show Judd's attempts. Probably early efforts when he began trying to capture Colin's techniques.

Sour milk flooded the counter, and Sage avoided a puddle on the floor. "Whew! That'll smell good when he gets back—if he comes back."

"No kidding. But it could be that person wasn't Judd. If that's the case, our visitor was probably here just after Judd left," Alex said. "Or, maybe Judd left in a rage or just plain walked out the door and found another place to hang out."

"That might answer the mess in the kitchen," Sage said. "All this seems jumbled. I'm trying to cover all the bases."

"Could it be Judd in a rage? Is this an artistic trait? Seems strange this place must have gone to hell in just a few weeks."

"But what's up with that? So far, the rest of the house looks pretty much like it did when we were kids." Sage ventured through the kitchen toward a small area she recalled as the living room. There was very little furniture—a worn green sofa that smelled like mildew, a floor lamp and a stack of old newspapers. Judd probably used them to start logs in the fireplace. Yet the pile was so damp it was difficult to decipher their dates.

"If Judd didn't do this, I can't imagine why someone else would toss the place," Alex mused. "That's unless Judd's in trouble and they're looking for something. Or maybe trying to make a statement. Either way, I'd say our friend has some issues elsewhere."

"Let's check out his studio." Sage pointed to the rutted trail winding from the back of the house. "Judd's made a track with his pickup so he can get supplies and his work back and forth. He works here when he's not in Colin's studio. I'm beginning to understand why."

The metal roof showed rust, and judging by their appearance, other sections had clearly been replaced. The building leaned slightly as if groaning from age.

"Reminds me of MT's outbuilding," Sage commented.

"And I suppose you know where this key is to?"

"Yup." She nudged aside a dark cobble with her foot. "Huh. No key."

"Maybe he wants to keep you out. Or somebody."

"Could be. This place is tight as a drum." She ran her hand along the upper door frame.

"Naw, that would be too easy." But a quick survey of nearby cobbles was futile.

"Okay, so you're the cop." Sage stepped back with spread arms. "Let's hear your guess."

"How about somewhere along the road? Or between here and the house? A little farther back but still easy to get to. And try not to disturb anything."

While Sage backtracked, Alex scouted behind the shed. A pile of broken and discarded shards littered the base of a small slope.

"Got it!" Sage's glee broke the silence. She hurried toward Alex while holding up a worn piece of metal. "Nailed to a tree over by the woodpile. There's an old fire circle. I doubt that's the usual hiding place—I just got lucky. And once again, Judd wasn't the cleverest."

"Give it here."

"Hey, wait a minute. Don't you need a warrant or something?"

"Not the way I work. Okay. Well, technically. Yes, probably."

"I love a straight answer," Sage said.

"If we find anything, then we'll worry about it."

Inside, the studio seemed oddly still compared to the usual hum of activity in Colin's domain. It lacked signs of ongoing production.

"Uh, oh…" Sage held up what looked like a very small stamp-like object. "This is totally weird—but it fits with what I was saying."

"What's weird?"

"It's Colin's stamp—remember? The little piece called a chop? Or a cartouche? I was telling you about them back at the gallery. It's the artist's personal stamp. It gets pressed into the bottom of the work before it's fired."

"It's from Colin's studio?"

"I don't think so. I'm guessing this is Judd's handiwork," Sage said. "See? It's not made very well. In fact, it's kind of sloppy. The edges around the stamp part are sort of fuzzy instead of sharp," Sage said.

"It's like you were thinking—and I'm sure you're right. He's counterfeiting your father's work."

"It wouldn't be that hard. I've seen apprentices learn skills from the experts. In some cases, it can be incredibly hard to pick out the so-called fakes. Just look how many times paintings have been faked. Forgeries have been around for centuries in the art world. Maybe more on canvas than with clay, but who knows? I'm not an expert. You'd have to ask my father—but of course, we can't."

"And look here." Alex pointed to a pile of boxes and packing materials. "Judd has a whole packing area set up so he can send out finished pieces."

"Huh." Sage leaned against a worktable. "We've been thinking he was shuffling stuff around in order to clean up Colin's studio. But maybe it wasn't that."

"Could he have hidden something? Or misplaced something?" Alex asked. "Maybe something that belonged to someone else? Do we know what pieces he took to Duluth for the show? I mean, if what we see here is any indication, this mess happened just a few hours ago—if that long. Looks like someone else was waiting for him to leave, too."

"Yeah. And I wonder if they're watching now." Sage stepped back from the window just enough so she wouldn't be seen from the outside. "I haven't caught any odd movement, and I scanned around the woods, too."

"If he's stamping your father's work—no, make that his own work—with your father's stamp, can we put that into some kind of timeline about when your father disappeared?"

"I'd say if that's the case, he may have been planning it for a while. At least several weeks. Months?" Sage flipped through a calendar on Judd's worktable. "He's marked dates for different steps—probably part of his own work schedule, and there seem to be other dates, too."

"Could those be related to that little stamp of your dad's?"

"You mean with one of my dad's real cartouches? Like when he was working? Good grief, I'm really getting confused. Like, who did what, where and when?"

"Hey, you're the expert," Alex said. He covered his face with his hands and rubbed his forehead.

Sage knew his patience was nearly gone. "We need to sort all this out—and pronto. I might be the pottery expert—well, not really, but you know what I mean. And you're the cop, so chill. He's stamping the greenware, which takes a while to dry, and if he's adding handles or whatever when it's leather dry, that takes some time too. Then there's the bisque firing and glazing. Good grief, it's confusing to calculate. Judd would be staggering them in the process with his own work, right? Guess having my father off somewhere makes it a lot easier for him, right? I wish Colin was doing his sculptures right now. That way, comparison wouldn't be part of the picture," Sage said.

"So, you've got your phone. Snap a few photos of the calendar. Then let's get out of here."

They tromped back to the car, Alex irritable and Sage baffled. Judd's plan—if one could call it that—seemed poorly designed. What were they overlooking? Alex's real job was to insinuate himself into the business plans of Holton Denys, not spend time playing detective with Sage.

"I think if Judd could just focus on the naïve buyers, it might be a little easier to keep himself out of trouble," she said. "Not that I'm encouraging it, you know. But in terms of anyone like me noticing fakes, he's taking a risk. He's using the same glazes and knows my dad's techniques."

"That happens a lot?"

"Online, it can be easy to sell knock-offs just by a photo," Sage said. "Kind of like an artist's dark web. And then some artists have protégés. Like Dad with Judd—really talented types that can pick up unique techniques. Sometimes, we might call them fakers. I guess it kind of depends on their skills. Some that steal Dad's techniques make pieces that can be difficult to discern."

* * *

"How has it felt to settle into Dad's studio? You don't get back here enough." Sage leaned behind her sister and gave Britta's shoulders a gentle hug. "So unpack your gear and get that wheel spinning!"

It was also an opportunity to focus on Judd's every move. He idled at the far end of the studio, likely furious at not hearing the sisters' discussion. Sage wondered how long he'd waited to find a capable mechanic.

Britta turned to take in the studio. "Every time I get home, there have been a few upgrades. I'm glad Dad's just tweaked the bare bones this time. I always want it to look the same—mostly."

Sage agreed. "It's expanded a bit in the back, but I like to walk in and know the place like it's always been. Colin shuffled some things so you can get to all the equipment up front, yet you still have your own area to work in."

"Perfect," Britta agreed. "It's almost total privacy. I see Dad left some glaze samples, too. I just wish he were here. I'm trying hard not to get totally panicked." She rested her elbows on the table and brushed an eye with the back of her hand. "Oops. Forgot to put my mask on." She turned to her sister. "Silicosis ain't for sissies—or however that goes. Get yours on, too."

Sage struggled until she'd managed to pull the loops over her ears.

"Anyway, this whole thing freaks me out," Britta fumed. "I'm focused on keeping my mind from wandering into bad places. Otherwise, I'd be a screaming maniac." She held one of her samples toward Sage and took a long breath to calm herself.

"I know, and I get it. Really. But we've got two of the best tactical brains on this—Alex and Jax. They're like super cops. I was wary, but right now, I'm convinced it's a better way to keep things quiet. You'll like them."

Britta broke in as if she hadn't heard her sister. "What do you think of this? It would give the plates some texture."

"Getting very close, I'd say." Sage held two tiles side by side. "Either one works. You're doing something different on the bowls?"

"Definitely. But I'm not there yet. The brown is a little too red for my taste. I want something to pick up the color of pine bark. Then maybe I can swirl in some black for texture. And dark green. Pines, you know?" Britta pulled a step ladder into place and reached toward a group of empty boxes. "I think there's still enough room up here. And for now, a little music would help. Where are those old CDs? This place needs to be pepped up."

"You got it," Sage said. "I saw some back on the shelves. Remember how Colin used to like them when we were kids? Said the music shook up his work." She wondered how long Judd would put up with Britta's musical choice. He continued to ravage cabinets and shelves. It seemed odd that he refused her help. A few days ago, he'd removed entire shelves of jars, then replaced them according to his preference. What was that about? She noted his quick movements. He never looked closely at the jars, just removed them from left to right, piece by piece.

"Want some help?"

Judd shook his head. "Need to move these higher. Don't use them right now."

To Sage, it was clear his real objective was something other than a neat studio. He paced, stopped as if to think, moved plastic buckets, peered into old cans, and bent over to drag a finger through a tub of ash.

She watched Judd, and Judd watched Britta. His movements were agitated, and he continued to shuffle jars and tools from one shelf to another. Sage kept track, hoping to determine what he was looking for—or what he hoped to hide. It was difficult to interpret his moves between cupboards, drawers and the highest shelves.

Britta's CD blasted out—and Judd's yell did as well. "What the hell kind of music is that? You expect me to work with that crap? It'll make me delirious."

I guess you never got into zydeco? I'd heard it now and then but never paid much attention. Crystal introduced me the last time I was here," Britta said. "But don't worry. We've got some old jazz standards after this round. They'll rattle your brains when we crank up the sound. Best background music. It's going most of the time at Loonatic's. Crystal says it makes for civility at the bar."

Britta looked toward Sage with only her eyes showing above her mask, then gave what sounded like a muffled hiss. "Is he on something? Let's try some of that zydeco." Britta turned the sound up a notch, winked at Sage, then spoke quietly through her mask. "I think we should wake him up with a little accordion and one of those scratchy things—rubboards, I think they're called?"

Judd continued his rant as he paced the studio. "It sounds like they're sawing their violins. That crap infiltrates your mind, you know? This isn't Mardi Gras."

As Britta's tolerance for Judd diminished, her artistic patience also was growing thin. Each round of her dish samples needed to be fired, cooled, then examined and compared. She conferred quietly with her sister. "I want a rich green. It also should be earthy looking— if that's even possible. I'm not sure what that stuff in the jar is, but it gives a better result with each test. It's not quite there yet. And I also want a version that's similar but lighter—like an earthy wash of celadon."

"Wouldn't Crayolas be a lot easier?" Sage noticed Britta's eyebrows draw together above the mask. "Seriously. Look. A lot of what you find in this studio is likely to give you an earthy color of some sort. Or at least a sort of natural, woodsy color. Why not allow for a little variation?"

"Right. But I'll know it when I see it. Hey, can you move that little Venus over here? Doesn't help to have a beautiful statue facing the wall. Maybe she'll inspire me." She held up the Mason jar. "I don't know what this is either, but there was another one back there too.

Remind me to put them both in the same place. Doesn't look like they get used much, so we can go for a higher shelf. There's so much stuff back there." She pointed to another bag. "And no label on this one. I thought Dad was so picky. Anyway, I grabbed a sample."

"That's how great artists are born." Sage grinned. "Want to bet what color it'll be?"

"Don't laugh. One of my profs just came back from China. He spent the entire summer trying to replicate an ancient glaze."

"And?"

"Well, he did, of course. And he put it in his notebook for experimenting again later. The best artists write up their results like scientists. Give me that scoop, and I'll add a little more."

* * *

Alex surveyed the studio. "I don't think Judd was cleaning up around here out of some sense of neatness," he said. "I think he was looking for something he didn't want us to know about."

"That sounds right," Britta said. "As far as that fit of rage he threw? He was 'cleaning' in order to cover up his search for God knows what. I think he was doing the same thing when I first got back here."

"Good chance," Alex said.

"And then later, we wondered if maybe Britta had dumped part of whatever it was into her glaze. Kind of makes you wonder, doesn't it?"

Alex looked perplexed—and maybe a little shocked—by Britta. This was Sage's sister? She was so agitated. He had trouble following her story, which seemed scrambled. Disjointed. He determined it was best to stick to the basics. "How did he act with you?" he asked.

"Weird. So, at first, he comes into the studio, and it's like I'm trespassing. Finally, he catches on. He's kind of garbling. 'You! You're Britta, right?' Like it was an interrogation. And he damn well knew who I was. Hell, we grew up together. Just trying to be some kind of jerk I guess."

She went on. "And I'm thinking, yeah, so? Well, he wants to make himself be in charge. Okay by me—up to a point. So, I say you're my sister. And what does he do? I mean, hey, I'm not hiding anything. I thought… what? He's going to maybe ask for my driver's license? He's just standing there, feet planted, arms crossed and scowling. I mean, I know he knows I'm supposed to be showing up on a Thursday. So, it's Friday, I lost my ride, not to mention my shipped crap, so okay? Is this some kind of a protected area? Do I need a special ID? He tells me Sage wasn't there right then. So is Two Harbors another country?"

Sage took a deep breath. Conversations with Britta—if they could be called that—sometimes left her spinning. Alex still stood, silent.

"So, I said, okay, I'll wait in the house. Sheesh, like I'm going to rob clay or something? Maybe decide to bake bread in the kilns? Then I figured hell no, I'll stand my ground, or it'll always be like this with him. I'm actually supposed to be working in here. I had that weird vibe. I'm surprised he didn't ask to see a passport before I could go into the house."

Sage smiled and refrained from rolling her eyes. She let her mind momentarily wander, and when she picked up the conversation again, she'd lost Britta's train of thought.

"…but he was oc-cu-pied, as he said, and couldn't be disturbed. Like I was going to talk his ear off or something? I'm perfectly capable of amusing myself. It looked like he was rearranging Dad's studio, who knows, what a weirdo. Seriously, it's like he was on something— or else really agitated. Like flying. And borderline creepy. He kept sneaking glances at me, and it felt sort of crawly. Like, did he expect me to be from another planet, or was he undressing me in his head? Geez, are all guys in Minnesota like this—hey, I know. No—But what's his problem? Did he get dumped on his head out of the crib? Weird looks at me, too. Creeped me out."

"How do you mean?" Sage asked. "The talking or the looking?"

"Not sure, kind of like he was on a private wavelength. Hey, I don't know, y'know?"

Sage frowned. It was hard to translate her sister. And had Alex been able to follow any of it?

* * *

104

Sage sat quietly in the canoe while a jumble of thoughts ran through her head. It was not one of those days with sparkling water and the smell of pine. Instead, a hint of smoke surrounded her, and the shoreline was cloaked with a fog-like haze.

Judd seemed confused about the last time he'd seen Colin. He was sure he'd waved when Colin left to pick up MT for their grocery trip. Trouble was, he was confused about what day that was. Great. That might end up a problem.

As usual, he refused to call her MT. Just plain stubborn, Sage thought. Or maybe a streak of defiance that lurked from his childhood. Could he have been calculating to determine the correct time and place or choosing a time that fit his needs? Given his dubious estimate, Judd would have meant he'd run into them the Tuesday before Sage headed home, a few days before Crystal had called from Colorado.

She rested her paddle across the gunwales and sat. What was it that seemed not quite right? She remembered watching her father grill hamburgers. It was a ridiculous, incongruous image. Fat hit the charcoal, the spits sending up plumes of smoke. Even after a shower, she took the lingering odor to bed. Clothing held the smoke even longer, and the memory returned just as strong.

She remembered Judd saying he'd been up by the fire. Saw Colin shooting photos. Checking out the fire's range of colors. Was going to tramp around looking at the smoke, too.

A trip back to the studio was in order, and Sage paddled back quickly over the smooth lake. She found Colin's barn jacket in its usual place, on a hook in the broom closet. There was plenty of dust but no smell of smoke in the closet—nor on Colin's jacket. Or, to be absolutely scientific about it, Sage thought, maybe there was a very, very slight smell. She had worn it the day before—for luck, and also because it gave her a feeling of closeness to her father. But there was no reason to think the jacket—or anyone wearing it—had been close to the heat of the fire.

Sage pulled out her phone. "Hey, can you hustle over here? I've stumbled onto something." She wasn't sure what Alex would make of her accidental discovery. Still, she was determined to reveal any scrap of information that might be useful.

Alex picked up the threadbare piece of clothing with two fingers. "What's this?"

"It's my father's lucky jacket. He wears it everywhere."

"Then you mean it would be unusual for him to take the canoe out without it?"

"Absolutely. He'd have it. And get this," she added. "It's got the faint smell of pipe smoke and a background odor of gasoline from the lawn mower—but no smoke from the fire. Or, at most, just a very slight tinge that's almost undetectable."

"At the very most—and I mean at the most—all it suggests is that Judd was lying. But if he was lying about that, what else is he lying about?"

* * *

Crystal tucked a list of daily specials into the menu folder. "Cold asparagus soup garnished with a dollop of what we're calling double pepper ice cream. You know, those gorgeous yellow bell peppers out in the garden? That works for summer, right? Mickey, my new kitchen guy, found a surplus of red bell peppers at the co-op, so I told him to go crazy. We charred them, then added a little grind of black pepper. Just a very, very quick scrape of it on top of the soup adds a kick and looks really jazzy." She stacked the menus on a table near the door. "If the fire gets too close or we have to shut down from smoke—or God forbid both—we'll need to pack up the fridge pronto. I'm trying to be creative along with good sense right now. At the same time, we should try to avoid leftovers."

"Anyway," Sage said, "You wanted to ponder—or is the correct word 'unravel'—the mystery of Judd? That might be an impossible task. If we haven't figured out his life plan so far, I doubt we're ever going to."

"Okay, I admit you're right. He seems so uptight—all the time. What's that about? I used to think he was bluffing, but I'm guessing there's some kind of mystery there we don't know about."

"Honestly, Crystal, he's so passive about where his life is going. Dad was always frustrated with him, but then Judd would have a stroke of genius, and it seemed like there was hope. It was like the father-son relationship Dad never had, but Judd never seemed to grow up. Bump into him at fifty, and he'll still be flying by the seat of his pants. He wants to be a brilliant artist, but there's no real drive there. I think he just liked being around Dad and riding his coattails."

"Well, creative is one thing, crazy another."

"You're saying my soup is weird?"

"Sorry—that was a segue toward Judd. Too much on my mind. I didn't mean to change the subject. But remember the summer after my freshman year? He turned up here wanting to be an apprentice. We were playmates as kids, but this was different. You know Colin. He was totally flattered. Sure, Judd worked hard for him, and he's become a reasonable artist. But he always wanted to take the easy way out."

Crystal nodded. "Sounds like he wants the thrill of the game, but he's not willing to invest the time or the emotion. We both know he's basically a skimmer."

"Right. He wants to be in my father's studio, and he acts like Colin is still there. Weird, isn't it? And I know he means well, at least I think so. But he's trying to subvert my emotions—my emotional involvement—by urging me to move on. Seriously? Move on if my father's still missing? Like if something dire has happened? Isn't that a little premature? I almost feel more sorry for him than I do myself. No, that's not right. But you see what I mean. Really, I'm trying to hold it together from one day to the next. As for Judd, he's got to be in total shock that he's suddenly alone and without his mentor. But emotional? Not so much."

"Stop. Now. Your attitude is slipping." She passed Sage a bar menu. "Quick. Order something that will bring back your tough side."

"Like a couple beers? Or is it too early?"

* * *

The sun rose along with signs of oppressive humidity. The rule of the day was to keep hydrated. Despite his bowl of water, Fabio panted near the standup freezer on Britta's porch. Clearly, he hoped Sage would open its door. Or Crystal might need something from the large commercial freezer in her kitchen. He'd been scolded many times by Sage, who hoped the health department wouldn't make a surprise visit. But certainly not in this weather—and Fabio knew the word "out."

Crystal drove off to Two Harbors, leaving MT in charge of prepping the dining room.

Sage crawled from bed, and headed for the studio, pausing outside to listen when she heard Britta's agitated voice. She stepped toward a side window, which gave a sheltered view toward the far end of the studio.

Britta was in the studio, furious and wary of Judd's behavior. "Good grief, you're back here after yesterday? How am I supposed to concentrate with your pacing? And stop tearing this place apart. Every time I look for something, it's not where it was before! I'm trying to work here, and you're messing with my process!"

Judd slammed cabinet doors and swiped his arm over a table crammed with glassware, pottery tools and cardboard boxes. His voice went wild. "Where is it?"

"Don't scream at me! I don't answer to screaming. Where's what?"

"You know what."

Britta tossed her head and let laughter overtake her. She realized she should be wary of Judd's temperament, but the ludicrous nature of his anger took over. "Remember that old comedy routine who's on first?" She immediately knew she had crossed the line of safety.

Judd leaped toward her, grabbed her shoulders and shook hard. Britta's head wobbled, and Sage felt the pain in her own neck. "You dumb shit. You know damn well what I'm talking about."

Sage stood, frozen. How could a simple discussion have gotten this far? She needed to intervene, but fear made her immobile.

The back of his hand smashed across Britta's right cheekbone, setting off a popping noise as the shock moved down her neck. She flailed, caught her foot on the leg of a worktable, and managed to take Judd with her. There was a muffled yet cracking sound as his head rebounded from the concrete floor. Sage cringed, feeling the contact in her imagination. In an instant, he was on his feet, heading for the rear door. "It's your word against mine here. Remember that. We're not finished."

"Word against what?" Britta yelled. "What on earth are you yelling about?"

Sage's voice flooded the studio. "Hey! What's going on?" She heard gasping. "Britta! Where are you?"

"Hey, I'm okay. Rattled. But okay." In a moment, she was back on her feet.

Sage pulled two faded camp chairs from across the room, opened them and ordered, "Sit." When she saw Britta was settled, she spoke quietly. "If we wondered before whether Judd had issues, I think we've resolved that question."

Britta nodded, closed her eyes and took long, deep breaths. Sage noticed her usually brash demeanor had faded. In fact, she seemed oddly disheartened.

Sage went on. "You know, we've had a lot of years to observe him. We've felt sorry for him. I don't think his mother was too attentive. And on top of that, his so-called father—should we call him, that?—up and left. A lot of things have been a battle for him. By that, I mean even his daily life. He thinks he's always got to be fighting—or taking on someone. The world has always been against him. He's one of those people who walk around with a cloud over his head."

"Sure. I know what you mean," Britta said. No grin yet, but she was responding.

"I remember a weird incident. We were about fifteen or so, and Mom took us to a church picnic. You were there."

"I sort of remember. I would have been around eleven."

"I introduced Judd to someone as Judson Pulley. He started to explain that Judson was an old family name. For some reason, I've always linked the name Judd to a tough guy. Maybe the name sounds kind of harsh. Or something like a loud noise. Judd. Thud. You know what I mean? And then there's the Pulley part. I also thought maybe his parents named him Judd to distract from Pulley—like they didn't think Pulley was a very cool name. Like something you'd find in a machine shop. Kind of low class, you know?"

You mean 'Joe Pulley' might still have been a tough one for a kid? Even though the first name was pretty much okay?"

"Right. Maybe he thought people's attention would be more on Judson's classiness and not focus so much on Pulley."

"That's strange but go on."

Sage took a long breath. "I'll never forget. Judd stretched himself up real tall and said something like 'Besides that, Pulley somehow reminds me of being dragged along on little wheels. You're always pulled around by someone else's ropes.'"

* * *

Sage was at Alex's door early.

"We know there's something going on in my father's studio. Has to be. Can you help me set up some trail cams?"

"Probably. But wait." He leaned against the door frame and crossed his arms. "Let's make the most of this. With luck, maybe we can force his hand. Let's actually tell him you're going to set up some trail cams."

"I'm not tracking. You mean, actually tell him I'm going to set up trail cams?" she repeated. "Oh, I think I get it. Tell him they'll be set up tomorrow, but really set them up today. That might be brilliant."

"It is brilliant. I can get Jax over in the next couple hours with some high-tech surveillance gear. My guess is Judd'll try to get in tonight before he thinks it's up and running. If so, the infrared will let us know. Whatever he's up to, you can bet he'll be back before long."

"Even after the episode with Britta?"

"Oh, yeah. He won't want to cross paths with her if she's around, I'm sure. And it'll be dark. All along, it's looked like there's something in there he wants. He'll be back for sure. Looks like whatever he's caught up in is making him crazy. That presents some interesting possibilities, doesn't it? He's in deep now and not ready to give up. He knows he's the odd man out. Colin isn't around—at least for now—and he knows I'd be up to date on his latest antics with Britta."

"Okay, it's a go. There's not much we can do on the outside on the spur of the moment, except I bet MT would let us borrow some trail cams in a pinch." He frowned, then continued. "She should be using them now, but there's no way to convince her. So, let's put them to work. By the time Judd recovers from yesterday's episode with Britta, we'll be set. Then you tell him you're going to put in a couple trail cams the next day. My guess is it'll send him flying. He'll be way more likely to get in tonight and do more looking."

By noon, the gear was in place, complete with a war room in Sage's old bedroom where they could monitor the studio. Even Fabio seemed keyed up.

Crystal would play decoy and drive off in Sage's car late in the afternoon—after Sage had chatted with Judd to set the trap. Crystal intended to be in Duluth for the weekend anyway, so that part of the ruse was easy.

Jax had already tested the equipment. It was primed for action. Other than the back light Sage left when she went out, the house was quiet.

Judd returned just before dark, none the wiser. "Hey what's up?" he asked while Sage carried fishing rods from the dock, Aside of edgy behavior and maybe a bad headache, he seemed his normal self.

"Lots. Just got a couple trail cams I'm going to set up tomorrow," Sage said. "I might be spooked—or crazy—but I'm pretty sure there's got to be some after-hours activity going on in the studio. I'm curious what it is. Until we find Colin, it's my job to keep tabs on this place."

* * *

"C'mon, man. We're ready," Jax said. "Let's get this dog and pony show on the road. Might not be hunting season, but I'm betting we bag ourselves a big one."

With the electronic equipment in place, it didn't take long for Sage to get Judd's attention. He must have set aside any thoughts about his incident with Britta.

"Seriously? Trail cams? I thought you'd have better things to do." Judd's voice seemed calm, but Sage was sure his mind was racing. "Life's pretty quiet out here."

"Yeah, right," Sage said. "You're not the one who played hide and seek in the gully not so long ago. I do have a lot on my plate, but if you could help me tomorrow, we could get set up faster. Besides, it would be easier to test with two people. Have you seen anything strange around here? I wonder if someone may be trying to find Colin's formulas."

* * *

Intermittent clouds drifted over the moon, helping to obscure the trail cams. Otherwise, the night was clear. With luck, a glint of anything other than total moonlight wouldn't upset the plan.

"So tell me how this works," Sage asked Alex.

"You should be asking Jax. I'm far from an expert. So don't get me fired if I'm not quite right."

"Okay, so?"

"I think I can come close. There's some kind of sensor." He took a long breath, hoping Sage wouldn't argue or ask questions. "It's kind of like an infra-red detector—a motion detector—that kicks in the camera if something gets in range." She seemed to be listening, so he went on. "It's the same kind of sensor they use in security cameras to show motion. Once it gets activated, the camera takes pictures or video. Some can even capture audio. That's the kind we've got."

It wasn't a long wait. A tall figure loomed near the studio door. He wore a black jacket. It was not Judd. Another figure, also dressed in a black jacket, emerged from the left of the frame.

"Who the hell is that?" Alex griped. "Move it in closer," he ordered. Still not Judd.

"They aren't saying anything, and it looks like they know their way around security cameras," Jax noted. "Every move looks like it's calculated. Good thing we put that gear out of direct view. Look. They're keeping their faces toward the door."

"What? These dudes are experienced at breaking and entering?" Sage whispered, forgetting she was completely out of hearing range.

"Headlights! Damn! Pick it up and let's move!" The voice was none she'd heard before.

"Who the hell is that?" Jax scowled toward the screen. "There's more going on here than we realize. Who was the idiot that said you should always look for the simplest explanation? So much for common knowledge. Simplicity it ain't."

* * *

Judd edged furtively around the corner and crept into a smaller dining room cramped with outmoded booths. Sure enough, there was Holton Denys, ensconced in the back, tucking into an omelet the size of a football. In one swift motion, Judd slid across the cracking upholstery and sneered.

The heavy smell of cheese and ham floated over the table toward Judd. Melted margarine left translucent blotches over Holton's financial page. The odor suggested the entire room was smeared with grease, not butter.

Holton's face flushed crimson. "What are you doing here? You know enough to keep away," he snarled. "We shouldn't be seen together. And I have no idea what you're talking about."

"It was clever of you to send me off on one of your errands and then break in," Judd said. "Oh, but wait—I mean, it was damn easy to just have your boys break in." He waited for a response from Holton. "And by the way, you don't look as classy as usual. Your bankbook a little sparce? Or is this a disguise to hide from the townsfolk?"

Judd could tell Holton's jaw was tightly clamped. "And by the way, how's your bank account lately?"

"Would that be a signal you can't handle your jobs?"

"If I recall, you stiffed me last time," Judd said. "I just want my due." He crossed his arms. "I figured it was safer to meet in public."

"Your due? Your due?" Holton repeated the words with a drawn-out snarl. "What the hell is that supposed to mean?" He rose partway from his seat and leaned over the table. From where he sat, Judd already detected tiny beads of sweat collecting along the man's hairline.

"I mean, you've used me, just like everyone else thinks they can. I expect reasonable payment for the risks I've incurred. And that's not to mention the value of my connections. I demand respect."

"Haven't I laid out all the requirements of your job? Your obligations? I have a big powwow coming up, and I'm sure as hell you won't be part of it."

"So is that what's missing from my hidden stash?" He shook his head and sighed as if speaking to a helpless child. "What is this, some damned therapy session?" Holton's question came as a muffled snarl. "Get out. Now."

"You expect me to cover your tracks and then be grateful I'm not getting reasonable compensation? I'll get out when I'm finished."

"That may be sooner than you think," Holton smirked, and his unnaturally white teeth oddly seemed to lure Judd forward like those of a stealthy cougar.

"Is that a threat?"

"My dear boy, I don't waste time with threats. I act."

Judd ignored him. "The way I figure, you owe me about ten grand." He swallowed to fight the dryness in his throat that threatened to cut off his speech. "And I'll take it in one payment."

"For what? Making a whole brick disappear?"

Judd looked at him dead on.

"You're right. I heard about that. And don't ask where it came from. You're lucky you didn't end up at the bottom of the lake with a few other people I know." Holton pressed his shoulders backward as if to dissipate the energy urging him to strike. "You haven't come close to nailing that piece of property. It's been one screw-up after another."

The sound of Holton's fist on the table made Judd start, and it caught the attention of other patrons. Still, he smiled back.

"Get your sorry ass out of here before I find someone to escort you."

"This is not finished," Judd hissed, and he tipped his cap. "Not by a long shot."

The breakfast crowd was thinning, and Judd was grateful there were fewer to hear. He spread his fingers, then angled his elbows, commanding more space and looking aggressive. He leaned forward and pushed up from the table, edging closer to the man across from him. "Got that, Holt?"

Denys looked momentarily surprised. "Holton to you. On second thought, make it Mr. Denys."

Again, Judd saw the face of a cougar guarding his den, preparing to strike. "Whatever." He looked directly at Holton. "Just get this. Don't. Mess. With. Me." With that, he pounded the table and stomped away.

* * *

"I want to know what you're up to," Sage demanded. She had bolstered her courage before visiting Holton's office.

"Simple. But I told you earlier, correct?" He leaned back in his chair and rested his feet on a large mahogany desk. "Will there be anything else? I've got real business to conduct." The so-called discussion—or power ploy—was clearly meant to intimidate her. In the background, soft music quietly floated through the office.

"You'll have to be more specific," he said, devoid of emotion and never taking his eyes from her. Sage struggled not to sneer. How totally, ridiculously inane at that moment. Her mind went back to their earlier meeting in Colin's studio. How absurd. She willed herself not to laugh.

Holton moved forward again, leaning over his desk. Clearly, this guy liked the psychological trick of taking up space. "Will that be all?" he asked. "Either step in or out. You're blocking my light."

Sage longed to laugh—then reminded herself to be more arrogant. She tilted her chin up, directed her gaze straight into his, and took a step forward. "You're quite the carpet bagger. And that's being charitable."

Holton stared back. "Let's get to it. I've got a business to run. What is it you want?"

A Colin knock-off was displayed at eye level on a shelf in an old display case with glass doors.

Sage stared at it, knowing it was a fake—and aware that he took it for real. Judd had pulled the wool over his eyes. What had Holton paid for it? Probably, or more likely, perhaps it was a "gift" from Judd to gain favor.

Holton rose from his desk and moved toward Sage. She unconsciously took a step backward, then mentally kicked herself for making what surely looked like an intimidating move.

"Do you like it? I have to admit, your father is truly an artist." His false smile broadened, showing radiant white teeth. They would not make a position in this town.

She stared at the forgery, holding back any comment. Why chance raising suspicion? Only an expert's eye would notice the difference. Colin had abandoned the glaze as lacking the character he sought. And the visual weight of the piece lacked the poise of Colin's work. It clearly was one of Judd's efforts. She wanted nothing more than to creep closer to examine the piece up close. But no, this wasn't the time. She needed to stifle her curiosity.

* * *

An oppressive blanket of stationary smoke had settled over the lake and the surrounding shoreline. Even in the heat, Sage shivered. Tension gripped her. The stillness of the air brought an uneasy quiet. She settled with Alex on one of the sun-bleached benches near the water. An overturned canoe made an improvised footrest. The lapping of the lake against the shore seemed like the slow ticking of a clock.

"What do you think about the attack on MT? I mean, why?" Sage settled back. "I feel like we were guided to her place."

"There you go again." This time, Alex knew it was wise to smile at Sage. "It's hard to tell at this point. And no, don't bring some kind of supernatural guidance into it. We knew we had to touch bases with her—in the best case to see what more she knew." He pulled his fingers through his hair and let out an extended sigh of exhaustion. "Luckily, we got there in the nick of time." He toed an agate near his foot. "I'd like to say the attack was meant as a warning. Unfortunately, we turned up just late enough to have them knock her silly. They threw a tarp over her, and hoped we'd miss finding her— like for a long time."

Sage gave a solemn nod. "I try not to picture that."

"In truth, the whole effort was probably meant to be… what should I say? Meant to be real? If it weren't for Colin's disappearance, MT wouldn't have sensed something amiss with Wats, too." Alex looked up. "Remember she said he had a habit of wandering off? Could be hints of oncoming dementia. But then she backtracked on that thought and wasn't so sure. It's a damn scramble of maybes and ifs."

"But if that's the case, couldn't they just try to make it look like she'd had an accident?"

He paused to sort his thoughts, then went on. "I wouldn't be surprised if they were trying to shut her up. You know, she can be everywhere at once, and she's always sharp. My guess is they were trying to create an accident for her. But then they messed it up—at just about the right time when we appeared on the scene."

Sage closed her eyes. "They probably saw us heading toward her place from down the road. They had to abandon the plot quickly. And, now, they've got to be thinking about what a farce their effort was."

"Sure. They couldn't even successfully get rid of her, and now she knows damn well she's in trouble. These guys don't like to have their plans foiled—and we clearly did that. Now she knows to keep the eyes in the back of her head wide open. Don't say anything, but I've arranged for her to have some protection. I'm hoping she won't see them and grab a pitchfork."

Sage nodded. "Look. We're not dealing with geniuses here. We've got the advantage of hindsight, but these moron crooks are making it up as they go along. They're drug-addled idiots. I don't think we can give them a lot of credit for thinking ahead. Given their first choice, you're saying they would have made their visit to MT look like some kind of fatal accident. But then we crashed the party, and they weren't expecting that. We came rolling up the driveway, and all of a sudden, their game plan had to be changed, right?"

"And all this is complicated by the fact that, as far as they're concerned, we don't know of any connection between your father's disappearance and Watson's. That old guy had a good cover, given his potential dementia. Too bad he didn't leave MT a note about what he was planning to do that morning."

"That would be a stretch, wouldn't it?" Sage frowned as she pictured Watson outlining his plan for the day. "Most guys wouldn't think that far ahead. Sorry. Make that older guys."

Alex dropped his feet and motioned toward the boat shed. "Want a cold one? I stashed some in the fridge. I'm not officially on the clock right now, so you may as well join me."

"Twist my arm. Okay, so you think even though they have no idea we found the tooth, they'd prefer to have MT think her husband just wandered off in a state of dementia? As opposed to him stumbling on something he shouldn't have seen?"

"I'd say that's likely. I get the impression old Watson was a shrewd guy, potential dementia or not. He knew what he saw—or heard—or whatever. It was too dangerous for them to let him come back with a story. Even one that could have been blamed on an old guy with a screw loose."

"Hey, that's not fair!" Sage said. "He was a genius of an old guy. Give him some credit. He knew what was up ninety-nine percent of the time, and he'd certainly be tracking the course of the fire if he could. Same with this crazy Colin mess."

Not willing to debate, Alex went on. "Was—or is—MT's place in line with the fire? That could have saved them a lot of trouble. I'm surprised someone didn't try to light a match at night if they really wanted her—or Watson—out of the picture."

"Maybe. But for now, we need to watch the wind's course. Sometimes it's tough to keep track," Sage said. "It can get unpredictable really fast. We're really lucky to have firefighters and planes working to douse the thing. Looks like right now they're not so much tracking areas for burning buildings—just vegetation. Massive vegetation. Especially if it's dry."

She scanned the sky. "That also means trees. That's a terrible thought. Believe me, we can't count on anything. I've grown up with the whims of fire all my life. Luckily, MT's got neighbors reasonably close. Depending on wind, there could be evacuations." She took a long breath. "I've been calling to keep track of her every couple hours. Right now, she's not in a precarious spot. And she does have the car. Still, I wouldn't say she's out of the woods by a long shot."

"Out of the woods? Seriously?" He finally laughed. "Nice pun, but maybe not so good right now. She's lucky to have all of us keeping track of her. And we have no idea whether your dad is in a tough spot."

"In any case, it looks like we're surrounded by rookies, doesn't it?"

"Nope. Believe it or not, this mess is in the best hands around. I think we're the rookies."

* * *

Once again, Sage dug into her father's office, flung aside worn and gritty copies of *Ceramics Monthly* and moved about his tools and notebooks, hoping to catch a glimpse of something that would jar her mind or suggest a new avenue for discovery. Clouds of fine silt rose from Colin's worktables and shelves.

"Might help if you wore a mask," Crystal said, fanning her arms through the air. "Silicosis is for sissies."

"Right. I feel like I'm chewing this damn dust."

"Find anything?"

"No, but I have a feeling Colin might have sensed something going down. My mother played the psychic wanderer type, but he was the one who always seemed to have the sixth sense. I think I got it from both sides." Unlike her usual self, Sage followed with a chuckle to let Crystal know she was only half serious. "After all, we did find the box with Colin's message in it."

"Do you think he may have left another message or maybe more than one?" Crystal pulled out a tissue and tried to ward off a sneeze.

"Hard to know," Sage said. "I mean, Judd's been back and forth. He might have found something we don't know about. It's just that, at this point, I don't know where to start looking."

"Maybe think about things in here you both used. How about books or tools that had special significance? Even sentimental value. When the two of you worked, what would you go to first? When you sit in his chair, what would you look at? Is everything in its place? What about when he groused to you about cleaning up? What did you do?"

"Cripe, Crystal. How do I know? My mind is so boggled right now, I can barely think straight." She spread her fingers and ran them over her head, then let out a groan of frustration.

"Okay, so just let it float around in your head at night. Turn out the light and let it flow. Have a talk with him, and let him come into your space to tell you what he wants you to know."

"Hey. I'm supposed to be the one in touch with this stuff." Sage winked at her friend.

"I know. I'm just trying to push your bright little brain into gear. If you can either get relaxed enough or pissed off enough, you might mentally trip over something."

"Right. Okay, you're right. I think I just tripped." She beckoned to Crystal from across the room. "Come here. Something told me to check the closet again. Today Colin's jacket smells like smoke. We absolutely know it didn't when we checked before. And… someone doesn't know we already checked it."

"Wait, wait, wait." Crystal ran her fingers through her hair and shook her head. "You're getting ahead of me. Run that by me again."

"Okay. See if this makes sense," Sage said. "But now… now they're trying to imply that he really was around the fire. Clever way to throw us off, right? We know for sure Colin didn't get up close to the fire scene. And maybe that he disappeared even before the fire started—or before it got reasonably close."

"Brilliant, kid." Crystal smiled.

"They don't call me Sage for nuthin'. But people saw him driving around. Or… was that Judd driving around? I mean, I'm thinking Judd's hoax might have worked and spread farther than just copying his pottery."

"Yeah, but wow, that's a lot of work," Crystal said. "A lot of subterfuge, don't you think? And really, it's getting a little too complex for me to follow."

"But you might go that route if you're a little crazy and are getting a kick out of it. Right? Or think of this angle. Judd wears the jacket outside purposely to make it smell smokey." She checked the pockets. "Huh. A couple agates. Judd always picked up agates as a kid. Maybe he slipped up and didn't think about anyone checking Colin's pockets. Colin doesn't pick stuff up. I think there's a good chance Judd 'borrowed' the jacket to set us all wondering."

"Okay." Crystal counted on her fingers. "You got here Thursday. The fire started… when? A little less than a week before? It's hard to know since we weren't right on the spot. So maybe you threw him off by showing up…"

"Yeah. He did seem surprised to see me."

Crystal went on. "You know, people say they saw your dad, and no one guessed he was missing... at first, only you and me. Wasn't very long, we had everyone keeping their eyes open. It seemed odd right away when you couldn't catch up with him from Colorado."

"But hey, the connections were a disaster..."

"Then you turned up and spoiled someone's game plan—or whatever it was. Funny how he—whomever he is—hasn't been driving around since you came, right?" She looked at Sage for confirmation. "Well, Judd's not all that smart—granted, it's sort of crazy to go to those efforts, and they sure don't fit together perfectly. The whole thing is kind of slipshod, isn't it?"

"Yeah," Sage agreed. "There definitely are some cracks—it doesn't have the kind of seamless fit of a really good mystery, does it? Or of a shrewd crook?" She watched the shadows of leaves play across the ceiling. Keeping the yard lights on had been Alex's idea—permanently. Funny how folks living in the country—make that the deep country—have always felt safe no matter what. Not so.

Why hadn't she thought of the lights as a kid? Especially when she couldn't sleep? She could watch nature's cinema from the best seat in the house.

That night, a grasshopper splayed his legs across the window, magnifying his body into a monster that grew to more than six inches on her ceiling. It crept slowly toward the shadow of a crosspiece in the window, then was swallowed by the image of a twisted branch. "Into the shadow play," she whispered.

"Come on, Colin. I still need your help. I've been here for days, and I'm still not getting anything from you. What are you trying to tell me?"

Sage also pondered her mother, who had read children's books to her daughter and friends. They all had special meanings—often about how to treat others. That seemed hard to imagine, considering she'd deserted her family, Sage thought. She'd always been more outgoing than her husband. While Colin worked, she held tea parties for her young daughters and their friends. Sometimes, they played guessing games, like "What am I thinking now?" And "I need to help you master your powers." It wasn't until later years that Sage realized the little girls were learning to help others and manage their own lives. And then there were those little tea parties.

Other times, they played with Colin's discarded jars or bowels. "What kind of animal would like to live here?" her mother would say. Or, "Look at this one. Its lid is like a little roof. I don't think there's enough room for you and me to fit inside." Sage recalled getting very excited along with her sister Britta. "Should we invite the little fairies to come outside?" her mother would say. "That way, we can all have tea together. And if you sing the right words, those little spirits will come back soon and visit us again!"

* * *

Alex paced, kicking a potsherd across the studio floor. "One piece? Just one piece? Where's the rest of it?"

"You mean our situation—like a metaphor?—or maybe just the rest of that vase?" She tried not to grin. "You sound angry."

"Well, yeah."

"Okay, so? Want to start this chat over again?"

"What is this garble you always spew? It's bits and pieces of trash. New-age crap that's been dead for a few decades now. There's not one coherent thread. But you toss it out as if it's your own personal dogma based on some idiotic educational philosophy, and you think it matters. That we all should listen and believe, but it's just scattered crap you manage to string together. There's no form, no logic, no cohesion. Oh, and believe me, I was taught cohesion—either at home or elsewhere."

He waited for a response from Sage. There wasn't one, so he went on.

"In my business, that's another way of saying it needs to make sense." He took a long breath. "Nope. Let me rephrase that. In my business, it's how you stay alive."

She stared, wide-eyed. "That's what you think of me? That I'm some kind of idiot mouthpiece?"

"Pretty much." There was a long pause as if he would try to backtrack. He shrugged his shoulders. "Look. Maybe I sound hostile."

"Hostile? I'd say so. And you look hostile. Your eyebrows are almost pressed together. I think if you scowled anymore, they'd make one straight line." Sage stood back to take a closer look. "I can tell your chin is locked up too. My mother scolded me for that. She said my face would get stuck and stay that way."

"I know you take it seriously," Alex said. "Or think you do. At some level. But look. You're kidding yourself. It's basically a sham, and you've even got yourself believing it. It shows you're a sensitive person, and that's about it."

"And you? Let's call you Big Man On Campground. Mr. BMOC? Your claim to serious discussion is quoting Elvis!"

"It's a goddamn cover, don't you get it? And it turns out to be a good one. Hell, I even like it. It rests my brain at night. Meanwhile, you're hiding behind this mindless crap."

"I research ancient cultures. It's not all excavating a city from 60 A.D. You know, there are stories and tales and legends that go with that. You have to get inside the heads of those people."

"There you go again."

"What?"

"You're spinning your own yarn outside the science that you so revere... cherry-picking the weird stuff as a cover for digging into the real knowledge."

"Oh, please. I didn't think you were capable of dumping such a load of garbage. You really have no clue. We're not just dusting off old potsherds. We're learning how they were used—like maybe what they held. Even something about what people might have thought. Or believed. I'm a seeker. And you're a slacker."

* * *

"Got an email that my lineage info's come back. I'm off to the post office to check things out." Sage waved off Crystal. "Catch you later." She smiled that it might bolster her chances of tormenting Judd.

Hunting for her family heritage served as a kind of head game, an intriguing exit from the reality of excavation, research, lab work, academic competition and whatever else influenced her life. And she had to admit, it was just plain fun, led to solid, captivating facts and it could uncover links to her mother.

At the post office, Sage carefully opened the manila envelope with her pocketknife. She scanned the results and then lowered the report with frustration.

"Thanks, Mom," she thought. Given the list of possibilities, it was hard to see signs of the exotic background she hoped for. There are no traces of Middle Eastern, South Asian, Hungarian, Portuguese, Mongolian, or even Swedish ancestry. But standing in the post office wouldn't help sort out endless options. When she'd whacked her head at that excavation in Israel a few years ago, had she badly jostled her brain? Couldn't she view some things just for amusement instead of turning them into events with significance? In her early teens, Sage tried hard to believe the mystical side could be real, but she allowed herself to adopt it with a passion. After all, it's what teenagers do. And her parents, especially her mother, had nurtured it. Being a hippie type came naturally. And Colin, living in a creative domain, couldn't have been happier.

What would this mean to her identity? Who in the world was she? Her father never claimed to have exotic blood in his background. It definitely was her mother. Had she been lying? Had she been lied to by someone else in the family? By her own mother? It was impossible to tell, but suddenly, everything felt false; every part of her personality felt phony, or worst of all, a gigantic lie. Who could she be? And how could she explain to everyone else why her background wasn't what she thought it was?

Good grief, girl. Get a grip. Take a breath and step back. Be glad you've been careful not to take it seriously among your colleagues. There was a sketch of the family tree, but it didn't go far back; nothing really substantive as far as inherited genes were concerned. So, stop this nonsense. You're supposed to be an educated woman.

She knew she was seriously overreacting. Still, she felt lost, totally confused. Like an orphan. But why? Her parents were real. Had her mother been faking this all along? Was it a juvenile game she'd played with her daughter? Was it meant to be cruel? To mislead

Sage throughout her life? How could a mother do this to her child? Perhaps it was something like the games her father played with her. There was always plenty of fantasy involved with those. Maybe this was her mother's attempt at a game she, too, could play. Or maybe she thought she was giving her daughter something to grasp onto from the maternal side of the family—to make up for what she wasn't getting from her father?

The wind had shifted, bringing a raspy feel to Sage's throat. Her eyes stung, and her nose itched. Although she kept the studio doors and windows closed, smoke managed to creep through minute spaces.

She should have hosed the roofs much earlier. It was too easy to ignore that task when parents were close by. Instead, she had evaded her experience with fires that crept so close—but maybe this one was just a temporary bluster. Breathing was hard, and common sense advised her to bail. Fabio looked miserable as he brought a paw to one eye. She pushed back her chair. "Okay, let's go, boy. Back to the house. We'll breathe better up there. And I'd better haul out the hose sooner than later."

"Oh, please, not yet. Let's have a little chat while you're here." Judd stood outside the studio, trying to appear calm, but his tense manner betrayed him. "Where's your sister? I've been looking for her." His voice revved as he talked, edging into barely controlled fury.

"She took off to help a friend, Judd. That argument you had frightened her."

His voice seemed to lurch an octave. "She called that an argument?"

This was not the Judd Sage knew. Not the boy she'd grown up with—or at least the way she'd thought of him then. In the stifling air, she imagined a cloying fog surrounding her. Her stomach signaled danger. "You bet," she said. "After her last experience with you, she was wary." Trying for a slow, calm voice, she asked, "What's up?"

"Glad I caught you here." He gave a smile that quickly turned to a leer. "Inside." He tapped his head toward the studio.

She eyed him warily. "You look…" she paused, "a little frazzled."

"Yeah. And you'll never guess why."

"Hmm?"

"Listen up," he barked. Sage snapped to attention. "I'm sick of everything."

"How's that?"

"Look. I've got Denys crawling down my back, and you haven't got a clue why," Judd screamed.

"Maybe I do."

"Not even likely." He lifted a platter from the table and slammed it to the floor.

Sage stood still, hoping not to intensify his rage.

"First of all, someone in this room stole my stuff. Okay, let me be clear. Your kid sister apparently has been testing how it works in a glaze. You know. For that restaurant project she's messing with."

"Ha! What was it doing in here? I mean, I didn't know you were into that sort of thing," Sage said.

"Forget that. For now, anyway. I've got bigger news for you."

Sage gauged her distance from the door. "What do you mean?" Slipping her body into a loose pose, she leaned against a work table, then slowly fingered her hair and tried to look bored.

The veins in Judd's throat stood out, and his neck twitched. He reached up to scratch his shoulder, and his neck twitched again. He seemed to be checking that it was still attached to his head. He gasped for breath and stepped closer.

"What is it with you?" Sage grumped.

"Hey, don't worry. Let's backtrack a bit. Just want to bring you up to date on a few things. Okay, Sis?"

"What are you talking about?"

He leaned closer. "Like I said. Thought it was time to clarify our relationship."

"I'm not following." Sage gripped the table. "What are you saying?"

"Aw, Sis, Sis, Sis," he leered at her.

Sage frowned and stared at him. "I'm not tracking."

He smirked. "You know. Same father, different mothers. You get that?"

Sage took a step backward, then cleared her throat. "When did this come up? I'm really not following you."

"Not sure I can make it more clear," Judd said.

By now, Sage had inched several feet away. "We'd hang out together... and... and you knew?"

"Yeah. Uh huh. I thought it was kind of—what? Exotic? Dangerous? Ha! Sis, I got a kick out of it. Could hardly keep it to myself. Not sure why I did." He took a step toward her.

She backed closer to the worktable and stared, baffled. Was some part of her life unraveling?

"Now you get it? That's right. Sorry, I don't mean to keep confusing you, half-sister." He pounded his head with the heel of his hand. "Half-sister!" he yelled as if trying to believe it himself. "Anyway, I digress. Your dad—our dad, was—no, is—the biggest jackass that's ever walked the earth."

"What?" Sage felt a sickening dizziness. "What's this about?" She wasn't sure where to focus. Everything he said sounded crazy. He's probably kidding, she told herself. Half-sister? Not likely. Maybe living nearby had triggered some kind of family fantasy? Did he want money? Did he want to change his name just for a publicity stunt?

"You never figured that out?" Judd asked. "About my mom and the dad we'd been sharing? Don't you think your own mother wondered when he slipped away now and then? Close as I can guess, it was around the time when my so-called 'real' dad went off looking for work. He never came back, ass that he was. Meanwhile, I was on the way, and Mom made everyone think Dad had gone off to find better work before I hatched. He went, all right. I think he just gave up."

Sage remained quiet. A black curtain seemed to move over her eyes. Still she didn't respond. Instead, she tried to gauge the easiest route to safety.

Judd continued. "Yeah, and I've waited for years. I wanted just the right moment to make him pay. Did he help her in any way? Nope. Nothing. And she was afraid."

Still no response from Sage, so he went on. "You know how things were back then. She left town, went to her family's old farm in

North Dakota. I was born, and we made a life there. When she died, I came back here to live with my grandmother—to get closer to the guy who knocked up my mother. But did I tell him? Are you kidding? Hell, no. I hung around the studio. Got to know him and learned his skills. Oh, yeah. He thought I was really talented. It's in the genes, you know? I had it all the time. He couldn't believe how fast I learned, and he almost made me part of the family—didn't know I always was. Then there was you," He snarled. "You prissy little thing and your asinine games. We hit it off, and suddenly, I was kind of a boyfriend. I liked that." He grinned at her and shrugged his shoulders. "You did, too. And as they say, the rest is history."

"Please." She was shaking, and her stomach churned. "This is insane. You can't be serious."

"Oh, I'm serious, all right. And you can bet I'm not through."

"What happened here?"

"What the hell do you mean?"

"With my dad. Something happened here, didn't it?"

"Okay, yeah. Back a month or so?" He thought for a moment. "Aw, hell. Just before you came back here, I guess."

"And? Then you told him?"

"At first, he didn't believe he was my father. He blew it off." Judd picked up a dinner plate and slammed it onto the floor. "Think the buyers will wonder why they got seven plates instead of eight?" Then he shifted gears and got off on that cocky-ass attitude. "He said I was nothing like my mother. Anyhow, Sure. I wanted him to know. Plus, he was on to me as far as Denys's operation."

"His operation? What operation?" Despite her panicked state, Sage gathered her wits enough to ask and to learn as much as she could.

"Oh, don't worry. I'll tell you. You see, I'm taking you down with me. Or let's say, before me. I've had it with your sick family—and your other-worldly bullshit. I've damn well had it!" He swept his hand across the worktable, sending one of Colin's platters to the floor. "Freaks you out, doesn't it? Well, it gets even more interesting. Denys has everyone fooled. And now he's trying to put the screws down on me."

"You're not making any sense. I don't care about Denys. You're all over the place with crazy talk. And exactly what are you saying about my father? He's given you a stable life with a solid skill. He's treated you like a son without even knowing."

Judd went on, ignoring her. "And by the way, I'm telling you, Holton has no interest in providing a cushy retreat for the rich folks. But you know, it's good if it looks that way because then it's easy to hide his intake. As they say, no one will be any the wiser."

"Intake? From what?" Sage's voice began to rise.

"Hey, you need a chill pill. That's a real option, you know." He winked at her. "Business is good. Lots of choices. I don't handle all of them personally, but that's no problema, as they say."

Sage felt queasy. Her hands shook, and a black curtain moved over her eyes. As her stomach rolled, she leaned against a table spread with bowls ready for bisque firing. In one sweep of her arm, several hit the floor.

"Hey, watch out, Sis. You don't mind if I call you that, right?"

Sage glanced back with a vacant look.

Judd went on. "There's the standard coke. But of course, the choices are many." He looked upward as if to consider more options. "Maybe benzos? That's benzodiazepine to you. What do you fancy, my dear? Oh, and I heard about something called dog crack. Or maybe it was dog biscuits. Not sure, but I'll bet your four-footed idiot would get a kick out of it. There's lots of stuff to play around with. Business is good." He tilted his head to ponder. "But then... I guess it always is."

"You can't be serious."

"Oh, but yes, I am. Denys is smart enough not to be directly involved, but he's also shrewd enough to let the profits pass through his coffer."

"You mean he's what... what do you call it... money laundering?"

"A catchy little term, isn't it? I didn't think you knew about those things." His laugh was hellish. "Then I managed to borrow some of the stuff. Those thugs of Denys went after my blood. I can't return it even if I wanted to because that ditz Britta thought it was something to mix in one of her damn glazes."

Sage's shock turned to fury. "What was it doing in here?"

"At first, this was a good place to hide it, except your father was smarter than I thought. And for a long time, he didn't let on. We all thought he was just an artist dweeb. But one day, he cornered me and demanded to know what was up. Said he was appalled that I'd turned on him when he'd treated me like a son. That's when I told him I was his son. He totally lost it. He came at me. I was still deciding whether to put an end to him. But then he swung at me."

By leaning against the table as he spoke, crossing and uncrossing her arms, and slightly twisting her heels, Sage managed to edge backward. She hoped there were no sand, chips or pieces of pottery that might give her away. There wasn't time to look for grit on the floor. She kept her eyes on Judd, hoping he'd be convinced she was engrossed in his story. To her surprise, she managed to breathe slowly, but the sweat on her face stung when it found her eyes.

Not sure what happened," he went on. "He looked kind of half there. Dazed by it all. He started to stumble, and that was exactly when I caught him square in the forehead." Judd gave a hoarse laugh. "Maybe it was a combination of both—his daze and my fist, but he fell backward. I'd really clocked him."

"Where is he?"

"Oh, sweet Sage," he cooed. "He's been here the entire time. You know that tooth you found in the woods?" He waited for a response from Sage. "That was Watson. Before I got scientific about the whole thing."

He went on, impressed with the ruse he was contriving. "You know, there's space in the kiln to throw in other crap as long as you do it piece by piece."

Sage's face turned from a red flush to white.

"I'll make this simple for you. Sure, you dig up a lot of worthless ancient pottery, but you're not a ceramic artist." He studied Sage's face. "So you see, first of all, I clocked him. Hard, you know? Then I gave your dear dad a couple trips through the kiln." He looked at Sage. "Hey, you following me? Anyhow, that made some stupendous bone ash."

Sage gripped the worktable and her hands shook.

"I've known beginners who have a hard time with glazes," Judd said. "Me, I just borrow from Colin." He grinned. "Hell, my stuff is mostly good as his."

Sage tried to steady herself. Judd took a long breath. "Like I said, that's how beginners learn all the tricks. Anyhow, I've always been intrigued." He pointed to a nearby table. "That glaze has kind of an eerie look about it. I'm not sure why."

He noticed Sage was taking long breaths. "Hey, I should get you a chair. Sorry. My mother was always big about that kind of stuff. Oh, and can I get you some wine? Red?" he smiled.

She tried to glance around the room without turning her head.

Judd went on. "Hard to know if anyone's all that serious about it. Clay, I mean. Never thought I'd be interested before. Too tricky, you know. So I just try to rehearse when our old dad isn't around. After all, he's the guy who wrote the book. I just hang out and absorb his skills. You know, like you do in a laboratory? Recording stuff in your notebook? I fiddled with adding his bone ash to my glaze. It took a while, but hell, I finally got what I wanted." He pointed to a large vase that stood on a shelf across the room. "Say 'hi' to our dad."

Sage looked across the room and stared at the vase.

"Yep, you guessed it. We had a private hot dog roast. But this time, right in the kiln. Hey, no big deal. He didn't feel a thing. He taught me to be absolutely precise about temperatures. Took a while, but I got it down pat. By the way, do you prefer saying Centigrade or Celsius?" He paused and smiled. "Don't worry. I know what I'm doing. I did pick up a lot from your—our—father. But hey, you look worried. It's all fine. It's just that he was too close to our operation. No need to look for him. He's right here. Been right here the whole time. Surely, you sensed his presence with your powers. Didn't you, favorite child? Check out that jar you were admiring last week. Old Colin is smiling right back at you." Judd sounded patient and self-assured. "Like I said, bone ash really does make an exceptional shade of red, don't you think?" He leered at Sage. "Good old dad never looked better."

Sage turned toward the corner of the studio. Her eyes fell on the urn, boldly displayed on its pedestal. "Good God, Judd, what have you done?" Her voice was raspy, and her eyes were like glass.

"Makes a nice glaze, doesn't he? I mean they. I even saved more for another piece. Do you think it's the same as from animal bone ash? We could do a scientific test. Although, if you prefer, we could just leave it this way."

"What, there's more?" Sage gripped the table.

"Oh, sure. There's a fair amount left. Wait—did you mean more of the story or more of the ash? Good thing Britta didn't find the rest of my stash. I crushed it quite nicely, and it's ready for use."

"Where?"

"In with the rest of his crap." With his hands on his hips, Judd leaned against the door jam. He gazed at the scarlet vase as if assessing his options. "I was thinking of carting that into town for the gallery opening. Good old Colin could hang out with his friends, and he could take in all the great things they have to say about him. What do you think? Should we toss him in the van and head in? Oh, but no. I think you'll be busy for a little while, and I'm not sure you'll make it into town. You're shaking. Are you cold? Could I do something to warm you up?" He turned his head toward the kiln. "But wait. No need to waste electricity right now. Saw some rope back there. And there's that wood kiln he just had to have. Can't imagine I didn't think of that in the first place. Much larger to load. But then Colin—oops, Dad—couldn't keep up with cutting all that wood. And hey. After the fire, we'll need to do some clearing... I mean *I'll* have to do some cutting. Too much work, maybe."

Judd edged toward her. Sage dodged behind the worktable where Fabio was choking and gagging. What had he swallowed now? It sounded like he was emptying a week's worth of food, and the familiar odor was more foul than usual. Judd took a step closer, oblivious. Sage moved backward and slipped on the mass of vomit. Fabio yelped. Judd came closer. She scrambled to find footing as the floor came upward to meet her. Her hand passed through the stinking, revolting slop.

Judd's face was trance-like. He gazed down on her with a contorted mask she'd never seen before. Threatening. Evil. Using her left hand for balance against the table leg, she pushed upward with her thighs, still holding the revolting mass. Just as Judd curled his lip and flashed an absurd grin, she pushed the slop into his face.

Time stopped for an excruciating second. His scream of shock terrified her. He reached toward her neck, then thought better as the putrid mess flowed over his face, into his sneering mouth and upward to his nostrils. He cursed and spit, which seemed to swell his rage. Taking a step backward, he flailed for balance on the slimy floor and his legs somehow propelled him forward. He bellowed as he charged for the door.

Who would—or could—believe the insanity Sage had just witnessed?

* * *

Alex was nowhere to be found. No doubt exploring some angle related to Holton Denys. Sage leaned back in Colin's chair, then assumed her usual position, feet on the desk. She realized she'd been duped. Put simply, Judd lacked the tenacity—and likely the ability—to spin such a bizarre yarn, much less pull it off. A shower and some food would help.

The screen door slammed. All trace of the peaceful morning was gone, replaced by the heavy stomp of boots and the wheezing and crackling of a smoker's cough. There stood Holton himself. The timing of his visit seemed unusual unless he had come simply to annoy her. Likely more pressure to sell her property.

"What the hell is that revolting smell?" Holton's eyes locked on Sage. "You actually slept in here?"

Her mind blanked as if a vacuum had sucked every rational thought from her head—or maybe all thought, for that matter. At that point, there was no way to tell one from another.

Holton swaggered toward her. "For a cunning businesswoman, you seem to have abandoned ship." At first, his gruff manner and mockery merely annoyed her. But it was more than that and intended to be. In truth, it was downright menacing, and the motive for his impromptu visit wasn't clear.

Given events since her return, Sage knew a studio could have potential weapons anywhere, and Holton was no artist. She did have an advantage.

Perhaps at his high level of stress, Holton could be lured into a mistake. She did have an advantage to contemplate a move. There had been a long fettling knife near the close edge, but there was no way to feel for it behind her. As a temporary fix, Sage called out the window to Fabio. "Hey, stay away from the water. And get back here!"

"Don't try anything," Holton snarled. "Here's the part where they say, 'stay where you are, and you won't get hurt.' But we both know that's not the case, don't we? You. Will. Pay," he said. "We've had this cat-and-mouse game going since you got here, and I'm full of it. You are shit out of luck, and it's the end of the line for you, baby."

Despite the danger, Sage couldn't help mocking. "You sound like a bad 1940s movie. Anything else before you tie me to the tracks?" She had to think fast. What was behind her on the table? Her hip nudged a pan of water and muddy slip. Holton took a step closer.

Her instinct took over. "Dad!" she feigned, focusing her eyes to the left and slightly behind Holton. The distraction worked. The trajectory of muddy sludge hit its mark dead on. Not a bad strike. Holton screamed in anger and pain as the wet slop and grit hit square in his eyes. He stumbled, then dropped to his knees, hands slipping along the floor. Sage gave him a hard kick for good measure.

"Don't worry, *mister* Denys," Sage cooed. "At least it wasn't acid. Dad used to keep that around here, too. Consider yourself lucky. And don't forget to shut the door when you leave."

Sage pulled her phone from her pocket. Very low on charge. She scrambled for Colin's phone in his desk drawer. "Hey. Alex. Need your help. Pronto. Get help. Denys just left here, and they might want to pay a stern visit to him. Seems he's taken to threatening me." She paused. "I'm not sure what got him going like that. I thought he just wanted to make me think everything was a land purchase kind of thing. Was I wrong."

"Let me get Jax over there pronto to have a so-called chat with Denys. I'd like to stay in the background for a while yet. If we can rattle Denys enough, he might cool down and accidentally drop some info—if it seems in his favor. I know Colin is somehow caught up in this; my gut says he's probably part of the sideline."

Sage sighed.

"I know. It seems crazy to ask you to go along with this. But try to trust me. I've seen it before. So—only if you're okay with it. Meanwhile, I'll hustle over, and you can get me up to speed."

* * *

Sage parked in MT's driveway. "Hey, you around?" She headed for MT's door, not wanting to alarm her, yet announcing her presence. She found her friend out back, pinning sheets to the clothesline. "We've got to get you a dryer before winter. No sense freezing your sheets—or yourself for that matter."

"Had the old one going a couple weeks ago when the smoke was so bad. But now, look! They're blowin' in the wind, and the smoke's headed the other direction—least for now."

"You're not worried your friends might show up again?" Sage scowled. "You're probably taking your chances being out here."

"What? Those thugs? I doubt it after their last visit. They're probably nursing their wounds." MT's feisty attitude never failed.

Still, Sage cautioned, "You know, you don't need to prove anything to those guys."

MT reached for a pillowcase.

"Hey, are you listening to me?" Sage stomped toward her friend, who pulled her favorite green and yellow plaid shirt from the basket. She grabbed two clothespins. "You know it scares me that you're out here alone."

MT raised a fist and shook it at Sage. "Fear doesn't get you anywhere, you know?" Then, with her best irritating sneer, "Just let 'em try."

"I give up. You're teasing me, right? I hope when I'm your age I have half your spunk."

MT's mood abruptly changed, and she moved to hug Sage. "Aw, honey, I know you love me. And I am careful—got eyes in the back of my head. I just can't stay cooped up all the time. Grab that basket and come inside. Looks like you need some iced tea."

Sage lifted the basket and noticed a shirt belonging to Wats. It was one way of keeping him close.

"Wats and I always moved as one piece. Like we were the same person. Is that kind of out of style these days?" MT asked. "Somehow I get the idea everyone's supposed to be independent. The hell with them." She took a long breath and went on. "I could feel for him, and that day when he didn't come back, I felt it. I did."

"You're beginning to sound like the way I think." Sage gave a gentle squeeze to MT's hand. Its blue veins stood out, surrounded by slack and wrinkled skin, while her own were smooth and firm,

"Oh, no, dear, no. You wouldn't have this skill unless you'd been with someone for years. Like Wats and I were."

"Seems you're the one with the well-developed mind-body connection, not me."

"That may be right. If so, I got it on my own, not like you claimed it from your mother."

Sage grinned and grasped her friend's hands. They were dry and cracked. "Well, MT, you've got one on me there. I do like to entertain that thought. Whether I've got it or not, it keeps people on their toes around me."

"No, no. We can both have it, just in different ways. I mean you with your mother and me with Wats—and whenever else I need to." She grinned. "It's all around us, you know. And just because I have it doesn't mean you can't... or that you can't have it in a different way. We just put our own spin on it. It's like we all fit into our own environment. We adapt.

"You think maybe we inherit some of this stuff?"

MT gave one of her familiar cackles, although it was more subdued than usual. "Who knows? And you know what? This could all be crap, I'm telling you. Don't look so serious!" She went on. "In any case, I did 'get' Wats in a way that astounded him. I truly think I knew the moment he was gone... the moment he took his last breath. Can I say this? I don't think your mother and Colin had that. They weren't symbiotic. And maybe that's what was at the root of their issues... hmmm?" She shifted in her chair, then rested her chin on a fist to settle her thoughts. She was in another place.

Sage was sure she was trying to compare her life with Wats to the enigmatic bond of Sage's parents. "There's no way you can relate your two lives, MT, just because you knew her." Sage understood what the older woman meant, but MT's explanation went on in her own language and with her own vision. Sage struggled to follow her logic, if indeed that's what it was.

"But what if I try to put it in artistic terms?" MT went on. "After all, I've spent a lot of time in your father's studio."

Sage wasn't convinced, but she nodded. "Yes, but do you think you might be over-analyzing?"

"All right, look at it this way. Your father's in his studio. Why is the foot on this or that bowl different from the others? It's because maybe he had a crick in his neck... because he had one cup of coffee instead of two." She stopped momentarily to watch Sage's face. "You want everything in life to fit—it's like wanting all art to be planned. My girl—change is all around us. It's everywhere. Look at the world around you. Fire. Drought. Flood. Or a tree falls across your path. Listen, girl. You know change. Your mother knew change—or what we're seeing as upheaval. She didn't do a good job living with it, mind you, but how was she to know? Your father did his thing, and she did hers. But mostly, she wished she could keep up with him, fit in with him... adapt to him. She couldn't, and that was her downfall. She would have been so much better off if she hadn't even tried."

Sage stared at MT. Her head was spinning as she listened.

"Today's woman would have given up," MT went on. "But then where would you be? Back then, I think more people made sacrifices, intentional or not."

"Do you mean people don't know if they're making sacrifices or that most don't make them and don't know they're not?"

MT grinned.

Either way, it was likely MT was right. Sadly right.

"Your parents were two people constantly butting their heads together. It's just that your father found a way to get away with it. He could manipulate the world better than your mother Dahlia could. Right? Do you see? She kept trying to make all the pieces fit and he kept wiggling the table. A few pieces stuck, but a lot of them bounced off and hit the floor. A few fell onto the hearth and turned to ash. And that old dog you had back then. Rex? I'll bet he even hid a few—or ate them. Can't have a whole puzzle without all the pieces. Same way with life."

She nodded as if she agreed with herself. "Too bad we can't read each other's minds. It all would be so much easier. Just think how alienated your parents probably were. Who could possibly have taught them to interact in a positive, logical, loving way?"

"You make it sound impersonal," Sage said.

"Not at all. I'm betting with her creative mind, your mother tried to set the course. Both had very creative minds. But trying to compete with your dad? I think she knew that was nigh unto impossible."

"Maybe that's why she liked taking those road trips with Britta and me," Sage said. "They were her getaway time. She could have jumped at the chance to borrow Colin's role. But instead, she acted more like she was one of us. Like we never thought of her as a mother, but instead more like a guide. I wish we could do it all again. Okay, then, what does all this mean?"

"Probably not a damn thing," MT laughed.

* * *

For a while, the smoke seemed closer, but maybe it was just a change in the breeze. Sage had rushed to pack more boxes and load more ceramics in her van. Exhausted and sweat-soaked, she kicked back in Colin's chair. There was a rustling outside the screen door. Groaning in pain and sitting upright, she shouted, "C'mon in, door's open."

The screen door slapped closed behind a slightly stooped woman. Sage looked up and slowly took in the figure: grayish hair made wiry wild by humidity, worn cotton plaid shirt of green and yellow like flowers in a field tied around her waist, and a beat-up straw hat hanging from a lariat around her neck. Even from a distance, Sage recognized the turquoise ring on the third finger of her right hand. Sweat stood on her face, and her arms looked to be covered by a coating of road dust.

"Well. It's Dahlia," Sage said. "The prodigal mother returns. To what do I owe this surprise? Oh, wait—make it this honor." She paused for a long breath. "Let me guess. You finally missed us? Or did you just get bored?" She gripped the arms of Colin's chair and felt a slight dizziness roll over her. There was a long pause as the two women surveyed each other. Is this what she'd look like when she was older? Sage felt her stomach lurch. At last, she spoke again.

"What do you want? I've told people you died, and the folks around here let me get away with that. If they have their own theories, it's okay as long as they leave me alone and don't mention them."

"I sensed something was really wrong."

"Oh. So you suddenly had the urge to pop over and say hello? Check things out? You're finally here now?"

Fabio chose that moment to snort.

"Bullshit. There's been plenty wrong here for years. We could have used your so-called powers then. You'll forgive me if I don't fall on my knees and greet you."

"You don't want to know where I've been?" Dahlia looked frail. She rested a hand on a nearby chair.

"Not really. I gave up on that years ago. Same with the why part." Sage took a long breath. "And now that I think of it, I'm betting MT knew about the whole thing, right?"

"I knew she'd always be there for you."

"Give me a break." Sage slammed the desk. "That's a total copout."

"Could I sit for a bit, please?"

"Sure. Why not?" Sage waved her arm at a rickety chair across the room. "Help yourself."

Dahlia cleared her throat and took a deep breath. "I wasn't what I said I was. I didn't have powers. You were young. I let you think I did because it gave us a close connection—and a path. It made us a mother and daughter—held us together from your father—even though the two of you got along."

"What was that about? You thought we wouldn't? And where the hell have you been? Should I call you Dahlia? It doesn't feel right to call you Mom. And are you saying I didn't really inherit those breathtaking powers you claim to have?"

Sage's mother lowered her head. "I've lost so much time."

"Wow. I'll have to change my personality now. You got a kick out of all the fantasy stuff you spewed. About exotic people and sleeping in ditches? I look back, and my biggest memory is the damn mosquitos—not something magical. Is that all you could come up with to make you stand out as a mother? I had a hoot tossing it around myself. Even told people I could bring you back if I wanted." She broke out in a laugh that sounded more like a sob. "For a while, I kept it around for humor—acting like I was special compared to the other kids. I must have needed that, don't you think?" Sage repeated. "I told people I had powers to bring you back. I was known for my momentous skills."

Dahlia sat motionless, staring at the floor as Sage went on. "I spin a hell of a yarn. Seems like a lot of the more gullible folks actually believed it. The others stared at me, probably full of pity that I was the emotionally destroyed kid whose mother ran off. And meanwhile, I was so trapped in your fantasy that I begged for that kiddie crystal ball for my birthday. Damn it, even my name seems idiotic."

"Don't be sarcastic. When you were younger, I always checked on you by way of MT."

"You seriously mean she knew? All the time? And you always checked on me? Until when? When I got to be about twelve?"

"I made her swear not to tell you."

"Why, but why? And why would she agree to do that?"

"I convinced her it was best. I would have killed myself if I'd stayed. She knew that."

"She's been like a mother to me. Like I wish you'd been. And now you have the nerve to come back?" Sage snapped. "And what does Colin know about this farce?"

"Your father and I were a poor match. But it always struck me he was a good father to you. So, what did he know about this? Essentially nothing—like the other folks around here—or you—for that matter."

"Essentially? What does that mean?"

"Okay—nothing." Dahlia drew a long breath.

"I always knew—hoped—you were alive, but yet you were dead to me. I can't believe MT went along with this."

"Well, she wasn't happy about it. Reamed me out, she did, but I convinced her to watch over you from afar. I know, at times, it tore her up." Dahlia stared straight at her daughter. "Do not get into this with her."

"And what were you doing all this time?

"Went south—Alabama, actually. Tried to make a new life. I couldn't bring myself to come back. I was useless. I couldn't live with your father, and I figured he didn't miss me much." Her voice wavered. "Nearly drove MT crazy at the time because she wanted a daughter. I let her be a backup mom. Then I just drifted farther and farther away—even from her. Far away in my head and far away from where I was. I totally lost track of time. It just seemed to go on and on. I was just oblivious to it all."

"And even Wats didn't know about this?"

"No. And then he up and disappeared? I gather she changed then?"

As if to stall for time—or perhaps to collect herself, Dahlia fussed to close a window. "It's going to rain," she flatly announced. "And by the way, exactly where is your father?"

Sage sunk back into her chair. "Rain? No, it's not. And Colin? We don't know."

"Off on one of his so-called seminars?"

"Like I said, we have no clue."

Dahlia seemed increasingly detached. She spoke, but a significant part of her mind appeared to be elsewhere. "The fire isn't as close as you think. It will stop."

Sage slapped the table. "You are delusional. This is a major fire!"

Her mother's naïve manner fueled Sage's anger. "Now you're going to call the shots? When I was a kid, I saw you pull this routine, but I didn't know what it meant. Right now, you talk like someone who says, 'Oh. Looks like it's going to rain tomorrow. We'll see if it gets the clothes wet.' Either help or get away from me. I don't need your bogus hocus pocus now. It's too late."

Sage stared at her mother straight on, hoping it would have an intimidating effect. "Oh, and by the way. While we're on that point, you think you can just pop up after all these years, and it's all just peachy? I mean, seriously? What makes you think that's okay? Can you even begin to fathom the pain you've caused?"

"I know. I mean, no, but I feel my own pain." Dahlia looked at her daughter as if to measure what Sage's response might be. "There were times I thought I couldn't make it through."

"That sounds selfish, considering what the rest of us went through. And Britta! She was just a grade-schooler. And you couldn't just think things over and come back?"

"No."

"What the hell was that about?"

"Pride… shame maybe. A lot of shame. I wasn't good enough. I knew that from your father. And I wasn't right in my head." Dahlia covered her eyes with her hands and began to cry softly.

"Oh, please," Sage snapped. "You were more than good enough for me! All I wanted was a mother to just be there."

"I know. And MT said…"

"Right—back to that. How could you begin to think MT would go along with this? How?"

"Like I was trying to tell you. I pretty much didn't give her a choice. I basically made her swear to silence."

"What kind of pact was that?"

"A very hard one. One I struggled to keep—and to enforce."

"Oh. Right… you communicated."

"I wasn't right in my head."

"You said that."

"And I was powerless to change it."

"Change what?"

"The illness. It was illness." She sounded as if she were trying to convince herself.

"We waited and waited. So what brings you back now?"

"MT. She pretty much demanded I come back. Threatened to send the police after me. I told her they wouldn't have any right to bring me back. Not now. But the guilt took over. There's no way I can even try to make things right."

"I guess I need to have a talk with MT."

"Please. No. This isn't the time. Not when she's had such a shock about Wats."

* * *

Sage had memorized the potholes in MT's driveway. This was the second visit in three days, and she'd also been checking in by phone. "I bet you could come up with a reason I stopped by again so soon. And in person."

"You mean the elephant in the room?" MT's shoulders crept up while she gazed at the floor.

"Right." Sage stood just inside the door, hands planted on her hips. Her usually warm voice had a frigid edge. "I had one of those feelings I get. And guess who came to call."

MT was silent. Finally, she raised her head. "Yes, and it's tough for me to explain. Especially since we've always been close."

"Are you referring to me or to my mother?"

The older woman took a long breath, and her response came slowly. "Come, sit. I'm so, so sorry." Tears now ran down her face. "Yes. I betrayed you. I knew your mother was alive for a few years after she left—all those times when you were saying she was dead. We kept in touch for a while, and then she stopped writing." She wiped a hand across her face.

"Go on." Sage was not about to make the discussion easy for MT.

"I wondered if she was hurt. Or if she'd been kidnapped. Maybe she'd had some sort of breakdown. And then I tried to tell myself she just needed to get away for a while, and she'd be back eventually.'"

"You really believed that?"

"I might have, I mean, maybe. I really don't know. The honest me wanted to believe it, that's for sure. If I told this story to anyone, they'd say I was spinning a yarn—and also that I must have been crazy to let that happen—to go along with it, I mean." MT couldn't look Sage in the eye. "It's so unbelievable. I've felt like a criminal who'd kidnapped your mother, which in a way is what I did. I don't know what possessed me. If you told someone this story, they'd be hard-pressed to understand the 'why' of it."

Sage shook her head. "I love you, MT, but I can't imagine— or understand—what you were thinking. It's insane—like ethically criminal, don't you see? I couldn't make this stuff up. And my mother should have had better sense. She doesn't get off the hook for this."

"When did you see her?"

"Yesterday," Sage said. "She walked right into the studio. Right now, I think she's staying out of my way. Shame, maybe?" Sage let go of tears that had waited for decades. "This is so—so dark. She took away part of my life—a crucial part—and you let her. My God, you helped her!"

"I know... I know. I simply can't put the pieces together in a reasonable way—in any kind of way to make sense." With her head in her hands, MT couldn't look at Sage.

"Do you plan to see her? I mean, you'll probably bump into each other grocery shopping?"

The question took MT by surprise. "I can't tell. I mean, I don't know. I just don't." MT returned her face to her hands.

"MT, no one's going to believe this. And if not to you, people will come up to me. What am I supposed to do?"

There was no reply from MT, so Sage went on. "I don't know whether this is the highest form of—what? Insensitivity? Insanity? Cruelty? Maybe it's even criminal? I mean, you participated in keeping me away from my mother. What did she talk about when she was leaving—or thinking about leaving?"

"Nothing. Nothing, really. It wasn't like her at all." MT lifted her head, her eyes brimming with tears. "That was the strangest part. Like she was in a kind of trance. She asked me to check the refrigerator and make sure there was milk for you and Britta. Sometimes you make your peace on what's gone before if you can't quite mend what's facing you now. What I mean is, always plan beforehand so you have no regrets afterward. I know your parents didn't teach you that, but do you recall the saying that you should never let the sun set on your anger?"

Sage scowled. "That's from the Bible."

"I guess, but think about the words. They're poetic. Toss them around in your head and keep a wide perspective. Go past just anger. For me, it means to keep track of where you stand with people."

Sage nodded, still perplexed but wanting to see where the discussion would lead. "I think I did that with my father. Or I tried to do that with my father."

"Yes. Exactly." MT reached to put her hand over Sage's. "You did. That's why you two had all the puzzles, and games, and tricks. As long as you were living here, you two were current. And your father had a special way of making that so. Once you were gone, give him credit for his efforts to stay close to you."

Sage nodded. "He even kept it up on our phone sessions. I felt bad if we didn't talk in depth, but by that time I was older, and I pretty much had my own life—and language. But we definitely stayed close. Even though I felt we weren't always in touch, you're right, there was never any kind of divide between us. Is that like you and Watson?" Sage spoke slowly, not wanting to intrude on the older woman's grief.

"Dead on. Even when Wats wandered a bit, even when his mind wasn't totally with him, we still had an amazing connection. It was similar to what you see as a kind of inheritance from your mother." MT gazed at Sage. "When Wats wandered off, there was never anything unsaid between us. We were always… up to date. Nothing was ever fuzzy in our heads. Terrible as it is, that makes the resolution of his end so much easier. That doesn't sound quite right, but you know what I mean."

"I wish it had been that way with Colin and my mother."

"Yes, of course. But it's none of your doing. You had a strong link with Colin and an equally strong one with your mother. But it wasn't your place as a child—even as an adult daughter— to find a way to fix the link between them. That's not for you to mourn." MT sat back in her chair to wait for Sage's reaction, unsure of what it would be.

"I think, in a certain way, my mother's so-called powers helped her care for herself, even without the kind of link we're talking about. That's how she kept my sister and me going. And also herself. No, she wasn't in the land of her dreams with my father, but together they made a place for Britta and me."

"Are any of us in the land of our dreams, as you call it? I mean, ever?" MT paused and leaned forward as if to ponder the rest of her response. "Maybe that idea itself sets us up for something that's beyond reality. Maybe what we see as everyday life is all we can ask. The rest is, and was, out of our control."

"You're saying neither my mother's so-called 'powers' or whatever I managed to have could really help me?"

"Well, yes and no. Can you live with that?" MT offered a tranquil half-smile.

"Do I have a choice?"

"Of course. Well, but maybe not if you plan to keep your sanity," MT tried to hold back a chuckle. "But maybe your discovery will be to take hold of your own personality and motivation. That's what we're calling special powers. And then, you're still wise enough to understand your human limitations. I mean, look. Love, human nature, survival, all those depend on everyone's unique powers, not just the ones we say your mother gave you. Not those from a special kind of ancestor. Look at some of the greatest people to save the world. I can't think of one who had those so-called powers similar to your mother, yet they saved us all in their own way. Take Gandhi, Madame Curie, Einstein—even Fred Rogers," she went on. "It's really a matter of all of us hanging in there together. What I'm saying is, don't discard or disregard those powers, but never consider them the be-all and end-all. They're not. We don't all have the same ones. As children, maybe we had a unique view of the world. And that becomes changed or shifts as we age and connect with others. And then maybe we learn to blend our powers with theirs. With daring and grit, we poke and jab our powers while we notice all that is going on far out around us. Everything from hunger to disease—and yes, to joy." MT took a long breath. "I do go on and on, don't I? At my age, I wish I could say I used those powers more. While we're young,

I think we should let them mingle to find their best effect. Your father is what I think of as someone who disrupts the spirit world. He turns it upside down. And your mother—well, I'm not entirely sure. I think she's always been kind of a spiritual expediter. A translator. Some people, like your mother, are as wise as the spirits. Less power, but more wisdom."

Sage wanted to scream, "Stop already!" Instead, she held her tongue, waiting for a break to jump back into the conversation. As far as she could tell, fate was made up of an inexplicable chain of random events.

"When I was young," Sage said, "the way I wanted to know my father was very simple, and it didn't work so well. I mean, I wanted a childhood like all the other kids. But my dad was different, and nothing could change that. Today, I know I'd never trade that unique childhood—even though sometimes I still feel like a child."

Sage then thought about Alex, caught up in a war zone, and the child who had crossed his path: one he'd befriended and with whom he'd formed a strong connection. And then how fate—or an offhanded fluke—had shattered everything. Not just for a moment but forever. It was a chain reaction of almost instantaneous incongruity, randomness, life gone crazy, and finally, utter chaos. Or what some would casually call the luck of the draw.

In her own life, fate had also been unusual, but Sage viewed it as kinder. Colin shaped it while her mother bent along like a young willow branch, doing her best to accommodate. How different would Dahlia's life have been in a serene setting? And as one child of two and eccentric parents, how had her own life become a reflection of theirs? Or did it? One is plopped into a place in life, and what happens from there on is out of their hands.

Crystal was another mystery, coming from the Deep South. As their friendship grew, Sage learned how Crystal's childhood and culture shaped her very different frame of reference. No wonder northern lifestyles often baffled her. Enough of the rambling mind, Sage told herself. All this deep thought might as well be going nowhere.

She looked at Fabio. "My dear boy, you have the ideal life. Food at will, freedom in the open air… what would you think of being a city dog while your mom worked away from home every day? Probably not much, right?" Fabio gave a perfectly timed groan. "That's what I thought. You're really a Northwoods pup, aren't you?"

* * *

Sage felt heat creep over her face, and her temples throbbed. She held a cold Fitger's against her neck for instant relief, then leaned back in her father's chair. It had been a long day. Good thing she was still young. Relatively. She rose, determined to help Alex, who was methodically probing every inch of the studio. In a dark corridor near the back door, she saw him in a large, rarely used storage area. He hovered on an ancient ladder, passing his pocket flashlight over rows of boxes stacked near the top of wide industrial shelving. His yelling came from the back door. "Who the hell are you, damn it?"

Sage heard him fling off the ladder. "Who was that?" She stood frozen while bolting footsteps led to a slap of the rear screen door. "Wasn't the door locked?"

"Stay here," Alex yelled. "He's got a head start."

A few moments later, he returned. "Damn it. There went my chance to talk to him. I would have jumped and grabbed him, but I was already hanging by one foot. Would have been a nasty flyer off the ladder. I've had it with all these prowlers—or whatever you call them."

"You're right," Sage said. "I mean the break-in. It's starting to feel routine. And I can't believe I said that."

She stepped back, trying to focus on the shelves. "Wow. I didn't think these would still be around." Sage reached for one of the boxes. "It's soft clay Colin got for my sister when she was young. Kiddie clay. She wanted to make pots, too, so he helped her form little bowls by hand. Pinch pots. And they wouldn't leave a broken mess if she dropped one."

Alex pointed to more of the same boxes farther back on the shelf. "I have one of those rare weird—and possibly lucky—feelings." He looked down at Sage. "Just how many boxes do you think your sister would need for playtime?" They were out of reach, but he stepped up to balance on top of the step ladder.

"If I start to go down, break my fall, okay?" There was a long pause before he spoke again. "Well, this is interesting. It looks like our friend Judd's been hoarding empty kiddie clay boxes and hiding his stash in them. Who would be looking way up there for toy clay—much less an illegal stash of whatever?"

"Hey, be careful," Sage said. "And get your mask on. Never thought I'd wear one for something other than COVID, but I'm glad to have it. Anyhow, I guess that stuff is bagged, but still, you'll be sorry if you get any on your clothes. Or up your nose. Or maybe you won't. Be sorry, that is. Anyhow, give me your pocket flashlight for a sec." In a dark back corner, she saw a nearly invisible, faint white outline on the concrete. It looked like it had been stenciled. "Way over in the corner, way far from the light. You'll want to see this."

"Huh." It suggested a box had dropped from the shelf and blasted out some of its powder.

"Doesn't that stuff come in some kind of bag?" Sage asked.

"Pretty sloppy crook, huh? Hang back. It never occurred to me I might need a mask. I wonder if Judd even noticed it."

Sage stepped back.

"It's like buying a five-pound bag of flour, then trying to get it home without white hands. Once we know more, we need to get this stuff out and the place cleaned. Or am I being naive? For right now, I think we just need to lock down that closet in the back. Jax can step in for that. There are guys who do that. Meanwhile, I'm thinking we should get a lock for this back closet. Or do we want to hold off on that and see if we can catch Judd red-handed? Looks like he's been scarce around here lately."

"One way or another, Judd's going to be back for this. He's probably the one I scared away earlier. Wouldn't want all this good stuff to get swallowed if the fire comes close, right? And by the way, you're going to have to keep Fabio away until the professionals decide what to do, which will be pronto. We don't want to tip off Judd, and we don't want any of this stuff around. Jax can set things up—whenever he shows."

"Just imagine," Sage laughed. "If the wind changes and this place burns, what do you think the smoke would be like around here?"

* * *

"Do I get a vote on this? And where are you two?" Jax entered the studio and scanned the large work area. "I go away for half an hour, and the world changes."

"Back here," Sage called. "That little room near the back door. Or the big closet. Whichever you like better."

"Half an hour? Don't try that bluff on me," Alex yelled back. "Okay. I'll get serious. What's up?"

"I was poking around at Crystal's place yesterday. You know, pretty much hanging around the bar. Even with my superior investigative techniques, I couldn't come up with anything." He waited for a witty response from Alex, but there was none. "So then I decided to scope out the area along that rock path. The one by the stream bed. You know, down by the playground where you spent the night."

"Not funny. Not at all." A flash of panic shot through Sage as she recalled her night in the same place.

"I had a good earful," Jax said. "It was a piece of good luck."

"Okay, get serious. Go on," Alex said.

"I stood outside while Britta and Judd were having a screaming match," Jax said. "The yelling carried. She used something of his to test in a glaze. When he found out, he went ballistic." Jax leaned against one of the potters' wheels and went on.

"So did you manage to catch anything?" Sage struggled to maintain her composure. The pieces were coming together.

Alex raised an eyebrow. "Could she really be clueless enough to get artsy with… something illegal?"

"Sure. Think of the context—or rather, the lack of it," Sage said. "Why would she think some stuff in a rectangular package would be anything other than what you'd add to a glaze? And in an art studio for God's sake? There was purposely no name on the packages—which doesn't surprise me. Clay sometimes comes that way. Take look on Amazon."

She could sense Jax was pondering. "Did Colin know about this? You definitely sure he wasn't part of it, right?"

"Seriously? Absolutely not. Not knowingly, anyway."

Jax looked from Sage to Alex and back. "But what if he somehow found out it was stashed here? What's the chance of that?" Jax looked from Sage to Alex and back. "I'm not as up to speed on all the scenarios here, but I'm getting some bad vibes for your dad."

"Yeah," Alex nodded. "Just brainstorming, but what if suddenly the jig was up, and someone decided your dad should have one last paddle in his canoe? And from what I see, we're already short of manpower with the damn fire."

Sage slumped against the worktable and reached for a chair. "I need to sit." She took a long breath. "Sure, we've had some unspoken suspicions, but I don't think I'm ready for the reality." She edged her body into the rolling desk chair, then dropped her head between her legs. The feeling of pulsing temples was gone, replaced by a feeling of lightness in her head and a room that spun on its foundation.

* * *

Sage half listened while she stacked Loonatic's menus. Crystal wiped a tabletop, then poured herself iced tea. "Wish we had some fresh mint like back home. Anyone want to make a quick trip?" she smiled. There was no response.

Alex brushed pretzel crumbs toward the floor, hoping no one would notice. "That fire could take us all out if we're not careful." Deep in thought, he rotated the bottle, sending rivers of condensation onto the bar. One sweaty ring anchored the first, then another and another. It was something to do, and he needed to rest his thoughts, call it what you will. Like a beer bottle Rorschach. He stiffened as the phone jumped in his pocket.

"Yeah?" His brows pulled together, and he turned away from Sage.

"Right. Okay, where?" There was a pause for directions. "On my way."

"What? What's happened?" Sage approached with eyes that were wide and wary.

"That was Jax. Sit down." He hadn't meant to be curt, but he waved her toward the table and helped her sink into a wicker chair. He almost whispered, but it still came out bluntly. "They have something."

151

"I'm going with you." She struggled to rise from the deep cushion. "Let me up."

"Later. I want you here for now. We don't know much, and it sounds like they're treating it as a crime scene. Besides… they won't let you in at this point. Crystal, can you take care of her? And by that, I mean keep her here?"

Sage's legs melted from beneath her, and she slid back into the chair.

"Sure. I need to be here for the cocktail hour, and she can either help or just sit. Can't you tell her more?"

Sage cut in. "It's a body. Right?"

"It could be any body. They're calling me because I'm here, and it looks suspicious. But I've learned not to jump ahead before I know what's up. At this point, it could be anybody."

Even with all that had happened in the last weeks, Sage felt an eerie combination of panic, shock and sadness. Learning the worst—if it were that—would hit hard. She clamped her teeth and blinked her eyes. "I'm good."

"Okay. I'm heading up the shore. And seriously, stay put." Could he trust her to do that? "There's a lot we don't know at this point."

"I couldn't follow you anyway," Sage moaned. Her hand trembled, and she pushed it further down the crack between the cushions.

"Hey, how about a glass of that Pinot you like so much? On the house, of course." Crystal sent a half-hearted smile.

"I don't think wine is such a great idea right now. But, yeah."

* * *

He gunned the Jeep onto gravel, headed toward Highway 61, then followed the shoreline north. "Heartbreak Hotel" throbbed in his head. The sky was cloudless, but another cloud—that of smoke—still filled the air. It had lingered so long it was almost part of the landscape.

His gut told him the victim was Colin—yet he hoped it wasn't. But who else? There were no other missing persons besides MT's husband, and he had other ideas about that. Eleven miles up the shore, he turned onto another gravel side road. Five minutes later, he pulled up behind a Cook County vehicle, then hobbled down the slope to a culvert and stream bed.

"Our guy here was getting impatient," Jax noted with a grin, tipping his head toward the body. "What took you?"

"Thanks for waiting." Alex scowled back.

"Thought you'd want a look before we took him for happy hour."

"You can skip the gallows humor." He didn't need—or want—much of a look. He steeled himself.

It wasn't Colin. The man showed obvious signs of a beating, but he clearly hadn't been in the ditch for long. He was tall—maybe a little over six feet—and his muddy, disheveled clothes included a purple Minnesota Vikings T-shirt. Alex exhaled. Aside from not looking like Colin's photo in the least, this dude was too young to be Sage's father. Besides, corpses didn't get taller after death, and the missing artist wouldn't be caught dead in such a garish shirt. Jax frowned as the bad pun ran through his mind. This part of the Northwoods was becoming dangerous territory.

"You guys done? Guess we can bag him."

Alex had a hunch the corpse was one of the crew that broke into Colin's studio or one who had stalked Sage. In a small town, the fewer strangers, the better. Chances were, he was responsible for both. Alex hoped the lab work would be revealing.

* * *

Back at Lunatics, the mood lightened. "I'm guessing he's the guy that played wipeout with me that night in the woods," Sage mused. "I don't know if that's good news or bad. It's only good if we're still holding out hope, and I'm pretty sure that's not the case. Are we?" She reached again for the wine bottle.

"A bit more wine?" Crystal quipped.

"Here, let me help," Alex ordered. "You been sharing this with anyone? There's not a whole lot left." He raised an eyebrow toward Sage. "I see you're still not too steady."

"Right." Sage cupped the wine glass with both hands, a purposeful departure from her habit of holding it just so by the stem. Feeling steady right now was out of the question, yet she needed to talk.

153

"In some ways, my father grew up. Colin Pan—you know, like Peter Pan? The kid who never grew up? But he played with me, he taught me, he cared for me. Some kids miss all that. I just wanted him to be a normal dad. But with the personality my mom had, he couldn't be any other way. He had to cope with her, and he didn't always do that well. Part of him ridiculed her, but I know another part respected her. He just couldn't come to overall terms with her. Geez, he wanted normal, too. We were just a bunch of misfits wishing we were normal."

"That's kind of harsh," Alex stepped in. "No one's family really fits the mold."

"Yeah, but we were way off the bell curve. Oh, sure, I know I loved—love—him. Like I said, we had great times. But I couldn't come to grips with a way to understand him. I think that's why, one way or another, I was always searching for him. Like maybe if I tried hard enough to dig up his personality, eventually I'd find the real guy. I don't know if that's even possible. And then to find that Judd is his son and my half-brother? My God, I wish I'd been with Colin when he learned that."

"And you might not be here today. I'd say Judd's rage was something beyond what we could comprehend. He could have triggered a stroke for your dad as easily as if he'd stabbed him in the heart. And then, he grew up mostly without a mother and with the real father he held the truth from. Talk about a master of manipulation."

"In his own way, Judd is a lot like my father, Sage said." She shook her head at Alex. "Sometimes the exact temperament. Totally focused, but mostly on himself. What a tangled mess. And to think we've struggled through all this madness on the way to the so-called truth." She topped off her wine glass again and went on.

"Britta said to call when I know something. I told her she should just stay up the shore. We can easily get her down here if we need to," Sage said. She was always alert to trouble and tried to shield me—funny, considering she's younger. But of course, right now she's in panic mode. Like why couldn't either of us have saved him from at least some of this mess?"

"Are you kidding? When? At five? Ten? Thirteen? No way."

"If anyone was watching, they'd say we existed in a mostly normal home. And then there'd be other times when we knew what our self-centered father was like. He never shielded us from his behaviors or what he thought. I guess lots of times we were too young to understand the adult conversations. No one could have been a better father but a worse husband. It would be interesting to know my mother's thoughts. Although I guess if he'd been a better husband, I would have had a different kind of respect for him as a father. Does that make sense?"

* * *

"I'm not sure we've seen everything on the Pulley property," Jax said. They stopped near a narrow, snaking hill with a battered wooden door along its side.

"I forgot about that. It's an old root cellar."

"Along that weird hill?" Jax asked. "Slanted inward?"

"I can tell you're a city boy. It's a little dugout room that stays cool in the summer. We sometimes have those. Summers, I mean."

"Amazing," Jax said as he stepped back to get a wider look.

"For sure. If you dug out a hole inside, it would be the perfect place to store the vegetables and apples you've grown all summer. It's tall enough to move around in, and the dirt doesn't fall in because there's some kind of board or screen above and on the sides."

"I'm guessing Judd's dad did the work," Alex said. "See over there? The wood looks pretty rotten. Judd would have been pretty young. And I doubt he'd take on a task like this when he was older."

"You're right," Sage agreed. "It would have been in use before Judd's father left. By bracing the sand and gravel on either side and maybe getting lucky to find a stable area of boulders or rock in the back, he had a roughly ten-foot square area. Then maybe he topped it off with corrugated roofing metal. It was the perfect space to store food that wouldn't fit in his family's small refrigerator. And I'm guessing it could also be a perfect summer fort for a kid."

"I need a better look at this architectural masterpiece." As they moved down the hill, Jax held back. "Where's that clanking coming from?" He scanned around him. "It's like a metallic rattle, but there's nothing out here. It comes and goes. I can barely hear it."

"Ssssh," Sage whispered and held up her hand. As they approached, there was muffled grunting linked in time with an odd pounding sound.

The three exchanged glances. Alex was the first to speak. "Either there's an animal trapped in there, or…"

"Or else it's Colin," Sage shrieked. She kicked the metal door. "Dad? Are you in there? Dad?"

"Hold on." Jax jerked Sage from the corrugated door. "We don't know how stable it is in there, do we? We don't want anything to shift."

"Colin! Can you hear me?" Alex yelled.

The muffled noise resumed, this time with what sounded like more energy.

"Don't move. Got that? Don't move!" Jax turned to Alex. "We've got a padlock here. Any ideas?"

Alex turned to Sage. "You're so good at finding keys, where's this one?"

For a moment, the activity stopped. Sage glared at Alex, then frantically patted each of the multiple pockets on her vest, hoping to find something—anything. She wailed, then dug deeper. "Here's a paint can opener. Or maybe a box cutter?"

"Both. Who knows what might work."

"Jax! Any way you can break up the board around the lock? We've got a sharp blade here."

"Send it over. Naw, wood's too thick—and I want to be careful about causing movement."

"Figured." Alex wiped away sweat with the back of his hand.

"Can opener!" he shouted to Sage, and she tossed it over.

One flick, and the lock opened.

"How'd you do that?"

"Rust," he grinned.

Jax helped Alex slowly pull the door open and dragged it carefully across the dusty path.

"Dad, thank God!" Sage screamed as she pushed through the opening. "Wait—shield his eyes! He's not used to light."

"Hey, like I said," Jax yelled. "Take it easy with that door!" He pulled sunglasses out of his pocket. "Never know when I'm going to need them."

She had never seen her father look worse. Even where clay—which he often called mud—was in generous supply, he'd managed to keep a debonair look. Now, his eyes looked like sand had been rubbed into them. His already sparse hair was matted in some places and formed erratic spikes in others. Sweat trailed down his face, combined with dirt, leaving streaks through reddish dust.

"Figured you'd find me one of these days," he croaked. "It's about time you showed up. I was hoping you'd do it while I was alive." Speaking took most of his energy, and he wobbled while trying to stand. "I was getting tired of humming the same old songs to myself." Colin's face was drawn, and he clearly was weak.

"This was Judd's doing, right?" Sage longed to wrap her arms around her father, but she feared his frail, unbalanced state.

"Oh, yeah. It started with him spilling his guts to me and went downhill from there."

"Here, drink," coaxed Alex. He held out a canteen and a collapsible cup. "Drink it all. I'll help you." As soon as the cup was empty, he refilled it. "I always keep it in my rucksack. Keep drinking, and let's get you out of here. Can you walk?"

"Yeah, just don't let go of me," Colin said. "This isn't the biggest kind of reunion party, but for sure it's the best I've ever had. Just let me get my land legs."

"Don't rush, Dad. We've got time," Sage urged while guiding him over the uneven ground. "Alex sent Judd off on an expedition a couple days ago. His car's not going to be much good as far as getting back. Not sure if he's managed to hitch a ride." She steered her father toward the path. "Good Lord. You've been without food and water. I don't like to think about that."

"Let's not. It'll take a while before I get all this out of my head. How long was I missing in action? A couple years?"

"Right now, I'm thinking just a little over two weeks," Alex said. "Good timing on our part, but I wish it'd been earlier. Looked like Judd brought you some so-called provisions. He got detained in Duluth due to a little car trouble."

While Sage and Alex led Colin to a grassy spot in the shade, Jax trekked back to retrieve his Jeep.

"Better not let me sit, or I'll never get up again, Colin said."

* * *

"Okay, Dad. Keep at it." Sage handed him a refilled water glass. "We want to see you drink the well dry. And I also want you to see a doctor."

"No way in hell. At least not until we get this mess solved."

Sage knew there was no use arguing. "You're saying every bit of this was Judd's work?"

"You bet. At first, he didn't show himself, and I wondered who it was and what was up. But it didn't take long to figure out. Just can't fathom how he planned it without help." Colin stopped a minute to shake his head over Judd's lack of skills. "He had me blindfolded, so I didn't know quite where I was. Once he had me locked up, he didn't seem particularly interested in keeping his cover. Early on, I was being a little uncooperative, and he downright snarled at me. Somehow, that pretty much gave his voice away. Then it went on with him spilling his guts. It went downhill from there—or underground, actually."

Sage bit her cheek to avoid laughing at her father's joke. "Can you get in the shower by yourself, or should I hold your hand? I'll close my eyes."

"Good, I'm good," he growled and went on. "That idiot's rage… hell. Yeah, our boy Judd spun quite a yarn about his tough life, and I'm sure he'll do it for you, too."

Sage didn't mention that Judd likely had his own version of a life story. And that they probably wouldn't be seeing much more of him. "I'll be glad when we get that interview with the law over with," she said.

"Don't know if I'm ready to revisit the studio until I get some rest. It would be like reliving that attack."

"Even though we'll talk with the cops, does it bother you to go over at least some of it? I'm still pretty much in the dark." Sage held both hands around her father's, squeezed them, then dropped her head on his shoulder.

"Not as much as I was."

That was good. His old humor was intact. "Hey, I'll put on a little of your favorite Chopin. Just settle back."

"Thanks. I'm still stiff—but not an invalid yet." She guided him to the sofa and helped him down. "Wait, I think I've had enough sitting for the rest of my life."

"What? You plan to pace around after all you've been through?"

"Nope. I'm gonna stretch out, my dear." He eased onto the couch, folded his arms behind his head, and raised his feet. The soft music of Arthur Rubenstein filled the background. "How'd you like to pull my boots off?"

As Sage tugged at his feet, she recalled soaking her own after that terrifying night in the woods. Was it mere days ago or a century? She lifted her father's legs, sat down under them and plopped them back onto her lap.

Colin took a long breath and closed his eyes.

Sage suspected some prompting might help. "How did he get you in the first place?"

"Like I said, he took me on in the studio. I'd asked him to work away from me for the next few weeks. I was looking for total quiet, and also—even more so—I wanted to dabble in a couple new techniques. I'm not a total idiot. Something told me I should keep the experimentation to myself. Call it an odd feeling. And I was right." He shifted on the sofa. "I'll show you the results when things settle down. Back in the beginning, I didn't hesitate teaching him the basics. But now? It's time for him to experiment on his own. He needs to find his own techniques—develop his own unique style. Anyway, it looks like he had a need to get me one way or another. I know now if Judd could cheat me—or heaven forbid, kill me—that's what he was after. Either suited his purposes. I wish I'd anticipated the whole thing ahead of time."

"Then I'm guessing he took you by surprise?" She kneaded his feet while speaking softly.

"A little more on the left foot, if you don't mind." He wagged his foot at her, then went on. "He came into the studio raging, wanting to pick a fight." Colin shook his head as if to fling the memory from his mind. "There's a big gap at this point—I'm hoping it comes back. The last thing I felt was dizziness and watching the floor come up to me." He rubbed his face. "I was dazed from the shock of it all. I hit my head going down." He pointed to the remains of a nasty gash. I don't remember all that much from the studio part.

"Wait." Sage moved to turn Colin's music down. Even Chopin, at low volume, interfered while she tried to absorb his retelling.

"Like I said. Sometimes, I get flashes, so I think it's coming back. I remember we had a war of words, and he told me who he was—my son. Back when I was in Japan studying Kintsugi, Emily and Simon moved to Boston, but they kept her mother's house here—the one Judd's in now. I didn't know Emily was pregnant, and I'm sure as hell not proud of it. She had the baby, then Simon had that industrial accident—if that's what it was. We were never sure. There were other stories, too, like he'd taken off somewhere out West. Sometime in all of this, she moved back here to the family place with her infant—Judd. It never occurred to me that he was my son."

"And the timing didn't seem strange?"

"Not really. Not then. It might now, but back then, I was even less astute than I am these days. Hate to say it, but hell, it never occurred to me. It pretty much went over my head—and artists are pretty self-involved anyway, aren't we?" Your mother and I stayed over longer in Japan, and Emily kept to herself and did odd jobs. My own life was pretty self-contained. Or self-absorbed." He looked at her with a raised eyebrow. "Too bad we can't go back, right?"

For the second time in two days, Sage felt a shudder as she imagined how bad things could have been.

"And there was no way to reason with him," Colin went on. "He'd finally snapped. Big time. Said something like he couldn't take the anger anymore." He looked up at his daughter, bewildered. "He wasn't himself over the last few months, but I never expected that level—that depth—of craziness. When I woke up, he'd tied me to a chair in the old sauna—the one out at his place." He opened his hands and shrugged his shoulders. "No idea how I got there. He kept taunting me—'what am I going to do with you?' I had a flash of thought that his comment was typical. So many times, he had trouble finishing things. Believe me, I know that's not funny." He went on. "It started smelling pretty ripe in there after a few days. I'm thinking that was around the time when he decided to move me elsewhere. I can't remember how many times he did that. Seemed odd to me that he'd take the trouble."

"You must have smelled pretty bad." Sage smiled and tried to lighten the conversation.

"Yeah. Right. He'd bring food fairly often, but sometimes he seemed to forget. Sometimes, he'd unchain me so I could walk for some exercise and see some light. Of course, I knew I couldn't get away from him, so I didn't try. My worst fear was that he'd leave me there or run off and forget about me. He was so adamant about my guilt. So angry... how I destroyed his mother's life and literally killed her. He'd pull up a stool and just rant. Sometimes it was like he was talking to himself, trying to make sense of his life. Other times, he just screamed, but he was careful not to draw attention to me. I was gagged a lot of the time. Believe me, that doesn't work very well when your head's clogged from pollen."

Sage struggled. Should she say something comforting? Maybe just nod? She wasn't sure she could speak, so she reached for his hand.

He went on. "He claimed she—Emily, that is—told him the whole story just before she died." He looked into Sage's face as if hoping she'd believe him.

"I know." Sage felt an overwhelming sadness. "I know," she whispered again.

"Times were different then." Her father had an odd, pleading look on his face as if his daughter could provide forgiveness. Sage wasn't sure times were all that different now.

Colin took another deep breath as if to regroup. "Then, for some reason, he moved me into an old shed. At first, I thought it was a storage pod. He had me blindfolded, but I'm pretty sure it was north of the old house. You must have missed the thing at the edge of his property."

"The day we went exploring?" She vaguely recalled the small structure near the area where she found the house key. "We came in from the east—where the old road used to be. Would be interesting to know if there were any signs that you'd been there."

"You didn't check out that shed?"

She sensed he was a little miffed that maybe she'd missed finding him.

"Had a corrugated roof like my more recent hideaway. On that stormy day a couple weeks ago, I was glad to at least hear the crashing noise."

"No, it wasn't there in the old days," Sage said. "And at that point, we were mostly interested in looking in the studio. We found your stamp. We figured Judd could sell his own work using your stamp."

"Huh. I must be getting old if he can slip that past me. Who knew he needed money?"

"I'm not sure he did. I think he did it just to satisfy his plan to somehow outdo you."

"Anyhow, it was hot in that dump of a building—or whatever it was. Ridiculous to call it a building. Miserable. Very little ventilation. Made me think of those poor guys crossing the border locked in trucks. I was sure I wouldn't come out alive."

Sage bent over and put a light kiss on his cheek.

"For the first few days, I sat chained in that chair again, day and night, wondering—hoping—he'd keep coming back with food. Wondering if he planned to kill me. I don't think he knew himself. Then he decided to let me lie on a mattress. But he kept those damned chains on."

"I'm surprised we didn't hear you—and that you didn't hear us—when we were out scouting around. Oh, Dad. I'm so sorry. We could've had you out a lot sooner."

"Ah, no. I think I was destined to serve my time. Besides, you wouldn't have found me there anyway. I think that's about when he moved me to the root cellar." He looked away and closed his eyes—but then glanced back and asked, "Where's he now?"

She wondered if she should even speculate. "Well, Alex put his crew on it. There's a couple possibilities. Holten's boys are probably gunning for him. After all, he's either got cash of theirs or who knows what else. And that's assuming the cash is really theirs." She thought for a moment. "Or if there's any left. And on top of that, there was that illegal substance of some sort. Considering the way Britta used it in her glaze, it's hard to know for sure. They're talking to her now." A half-smile spread across her lips. "Given the current chaos, she may have other career plans at this point—or maybe safer ones. But then, maybe not. She's pretty stubborn. I called her right after we found you, and she's on her way."

"That's good for her. Being stubborn, I mean."

"Well," Sage went on. "You always had a mind of your own... and a very independent life. Strange things like this happen to people like you. I mean, don't get me wrong, but you lived a fairly unconventional life, if that's the right thing to call it. You were off in your own head a lot. I don't mean to be—what—rude?"

"Go ahead. At this age, your old dad might learn something."

Sage decided to plunge in with a memory that never had faded.

"Okay. So, remember when we went to Buck Henderson's funeral? You sat in the church with your calculator and a notebook. I think maybe you were making what you called 'prototype test glazes.' You were so off in your own world that you never noticed the church ladies pointing at you and scowling."

"Really?" Colin slapped his leg and gave what seemed to Sage a proud laugh. "I don't remember, but that would be me, all right."

"I never understood if all that acting was on purpose or if it was really your personality, and you couldn't help it." At first, her comment seemed to float over his head, and he crossed his arms over his chest.

"I always know what I'm doing," he huffed.

"Don't be defensive. Being your daughter, I know."

* * *

"You hardly said a word when we got Colin back." Sage looked hard at Alex. "What were you thinking? It was like you were off and lost somewhere in your head."

163

"Okay. I'll bite." Alex seemed uncomfortable. "In some ways, your emotions make you a lucky person. For me, in most places—make that most situations—I don't feel anything. Well, that's not exactly true. I always feel like I'm lost on the bus."

Sage grinned, then felt guilty. "Well, think about this. It's how I see it. Some people never realize they don't feel anything. Like somehow their very soul is shut off. Turned off emotionally. Sometimes it happens when they're in new situations or new places. It could be from shock or even horror." She watched Alex tighten his jaw and stare. "They seem to just shut down and check out, she said."

"You're really good with the woo-woo talk."

She pushed on. "Think of it this way. If I were sitting on some kind of pier, say somewhere in the Mediterranean, I might be looking around and taking in all the things I'd never seen before—markets, ships, the smell of the air. My brain would file all that away as new stuff. I'd see totally amazing, incredible, fascinating things. But still, it wouldn't be like saying, 'Wow, Sage, do you feel this in your gut? Do you have a visceral connection?' And I'd think, 'not really, but this is different. I'm still totally captivated by all these wonders.' On the other hand, if you'd transport me to *my* country, where I have connections... and memories... I could sit out on the worst day and feel, refreshed... loved... part of all being. Does that make any sense?"

"No... it kind of goes around in circles."

"What? Seriously?" Sage shrieked.

"Listen," he said. "It's just babble. For me, you're too far inside your own head. That's not the way I think." He paused as if to arrange his thoughts. "I look outside, and there are trees and rocks."

Sage frowned and squinted at him. "See if I'm getting what you mean—you see the sun going down instead of seeing a really great sunset."

"Well, yeah. Kind of. It's there, but it's nothingness. What is that?"

"I hate to sound harsh," Sage said, "but that nothingness sounds like the kind of nothingness you've allowed. Almost like you can't be bothered. Or maybe it's some kind of a..."

He looked at her and grinned. "Well, I don't take that feeling of nothingness for nothing."

"There you go again."

"That was supposed to be funny. We've both had unusual lives. But in some ways, everyone has that. You never know when or where you're going to connect. You've had experiences I've never had. It's not a matter of being some kind of late bloomer, if that's what you're thinking. It's where you are and what you've been." He stopped for a moment. "Or what you are and where you've been. Now I'm not sure."

"You realize this talk is all nonsense, don't you? Really, it's partly that you've had such a rush of experiences—not all good—that you haven't had time to think between them. Mine were different. But yours were right there in your face, right?"

"Sounds about right." He looked away and took a long breath.

"Look," she said. "What you've told me you've experienced, on those beaches? The death? That's way worse than me digging up skeletons. I'm looking for ancient skeletons on one hand—digging for them—then once I'm back home, I'm looking for old skeletons from my life. And you know what? If you think about it, so is Judd. Trouble is, he's rattling around somewhere in his head, and he can't find his way out. God forbid anyone should crawl into the kind of mental pit he's in."

Alex took a long breath. "Speaking of pits..."

Sage went on. "I keep having dreams that I'm at some kind of high school dance. Maybe it's from the year Colin had a visiting faculty thing down in Minneapolis. He didn't teach on Fridays, so we'd sneak home to 'reality,' as he called it. I loved those weekends. I'd keep trying to find people I wanted to hang around with, but they were all off elsewhere. I could never figure that out. It's because I was trying to look 'desirable,' like someone a guy would want for a girlfriend, but no one was around. I'd walk circles around the same paths we have now, over and over, avoiding my room. I was always trying to find my 'place.' I don't think I ever did."

Alex still looked puzzled, but before she went on, Sage waited to see if he would respond. "You're looking at me in a weird way," she said. "I think it maybe means I was chasing dreams—or something like that? Not definable, but something that slips through your fingers."

He still seemed confused. "I don't feel much of that now, but despite your worldly 'adventures,' I see some of it in you. It sounds like you're looking for an easy way for me to see myself?"

"I'm not sure," Sage said.

He crossed his arms. "Well, it's not working."

"I think you have to cut loose of everything in your muddy, grainy head," Sage said. "You have to compare all those intriguing, mystifying, glorious places with the question of where do I want to be, whether I'm daydreaming or out there in real life?" She waited for a response. "What do I really want? And what can I do to make it real?"

"Like sorting through my brain," he said.

"Or your psyche. See, now you're getting it." Sage raised her fists as if to cheer. "Right now, what's popping into your brain?"

"I think I need to go back to the point where everything went so bad. The Mediterranean, or somewhere around there… but this time, a place that's gotten more serene. It's like some kind of pull. Like I need to go to one of those beaches. That beach. Maybe I have to put myself there again—to see and feel what happened. Maybe I always want that memory to guide my compassion." He took a long breath. "I'll never forget it, but I don't want it to kill me either."

Sage nodded. "It's a long trip, and you know it'll be tough. But I think you're saying there's no way around it, right?" He nodded and lowered his head into his hands.

"Don't worry about Qadri. He'll always have a place here. He knows us, and we've made him part of our families. Sure, he'll miss you, but he adores Jax, and it goes the other way too." She watched Alex take a long breath, then went on. "Those two will hang together a lot. In fact, Qadri'll probably get more attention than he needs from all of us. That'll be good right now."

Alex nodded, knowing Sage was right.

"MT stops by pretty often, and she'll spoil him rotten." Sage laughed. "That'll help him settle in with all of us, and we'll always know where he is."

"Good plan. The more he finds himself in a safe place, the better."

With the wind going in another direction, a damp, swampy aroma prevailed, and with the sun's heat, the air brewed a mixture of swamp muck, tea made of dry birch leaves, and water with a mineral scent evaporating from the surface of broken rock. Sage stopped briefly to inhale the rich, familiar scent mixture she knew so well. Her mind floated back to pieces of rock picked up and carried home, just to see what the inside looked like after a whack with her hammer. Her pocket magnifying glass opened a world of shining sheets of mica, jagged pieces of pink feldspar—or sometimes just the fine-grained black of a Precambrian basalt flow. On other forages, she picked wildflowers and gently laid them on tissue paper, then between the pages of a thick book she carried in her pack.

The outdoors was a glorious place to explore, and it was all hers. There had been a brief summer visit, home between academic commitments, when she retraced a drive far back from the shore, stopping to revisit a favorite hill of birch swooping toward Lake Superior. She recalled how, on a fall day, it had glowed with a spectacular light through golden leaves, casting pure yellowness in the midst of white birch trunks. In the center of her view sat two dilapidated wicker chairs resting alone in the glow. No sense of activity, no cabin. Why, oh, why hadn't she snapped a photo? When she returned several years later, the golden light wasn't as intense, and the chairs were gone. She always held those two visits as a symbol of how life's beautiful moments never last—or else maybe our minds trick us into believing a glorified image that was never quite there. But no, that vision was real. As golden as a mortal could imagine.

The memory of that day abruptly left, and her thoughts retreated to her current objective—to puzzle through the tangle of events that linked everyone around her. The overall picture seemed daunting. Her mother had returned from oblivion. Her father was slowly recovering physically and emotionally but still partly off in some oblivion of his own. He seemed mostly responsible and mentally in charge, the best parts of his personality returning slowly. During the times he seemed confused, Sage suspected he was wrestling with less pleasant reminders of his past. As long as there was slow improvement, she counted the overall situation good.

Then there was Alex, planning to take a second whack at his demons, hoping to win against them and reclaim his life—or perhaps create a new one. Crystal, fighting to grab and hold onto her "self," dodging a crazed husband who she hoped wouldn't discover her new life or set a trap that would force her back into the old one. Among the women, MT was truly the strongest and wisest, despite the emotional chaos she'd supported. *Please help me be like her*, Sage thought. And her sister Britta, a free spirit looking to shape her life. Finally, there was her mother Dahlia— still under observation, a nemesis for everyone. In the midst of disorder, Sage felt the weakest of all. Was chaos the only way life could be? Or could all the pieces eventually shake out into rational order?

* * *

Back in the studio, father and daughter pondered old times. "Maybe I was too free," he mused. "Being an artist can be like that. In my mind, I saw myself following that life. 'The Picasso of Clay' in the north woods of Minnesota."

Sage listened quietly, not wanting to break his train of thought.

"I wanted a reputation. To have people know me—not to be just another mediocre artist. Is that foolish?"

"No." Sage pondered what to say. "Not really, I guess."

"But I thought there were a million geniuses like me. If I couldn't stand out somehow… make my work different… where would I be?" He mused. "Then I'd just be one of those loose-living hippie guys out in the woods."

You were—or are, Sage thought to herself.

"I dreamt about the artist life, but your mother was practical." He looked at Sage as if hoping she'd understand—maybe even take his side. "She pretty much rained on my parade more than once. Or maybe she just wanted to be normal—so we all could fit in. You know, raise kids, take them to the zoo, make those little round cakes."

"Cupcakes," Sage said. "Anyway, she really tried to be on that path. Maybe she thought you didn't appreciate what she did—for all of us."

Colin sat quietly, so she went on.

"Did she feel she had no power? Or that she could never quite measure up?" Sage probed cautiously. "I think lots of times she felt like the lone person in the background."

"So you think I was off in my own world?" Colin asked. "I couldn't just set aside my talents, could I?"

"But that's my point! We played games I'll never forget. We paddled across one lake and followed the stream to the next. That was huge. We played with compasses and built fires. I like to think one of those games maybe saved both of our lives but at different times."

"Like that hidden box in the rafters? If you hadn't been so close—or make that so crazy—I can't imagine what we would have done to find you."

Colin sighed and nodded. "That really was a bit much, wasn't it?"

"Meanwhile, Mother's on-the-road-fantasy stories were as creative as your art. For sure, both of you were at opposite ends of a pretty complicated spectrum. We never met as a family in the middle. You took us to great places. Everyone loved your girls. The women even took us in their kitchens. I learned to bake breads from Santiago to somewhere, but you never were close. Yeah, we had great times together, but it was all play. I don't think we ever had a serious discussion in our lives. You were never a normal father, and Judd was my damn brother. Did mother know?"

"Of course not." Colin took a long breath as his eyes spanned the studio. "See how things have been rearranged—so to speak? It wouldn't be so bad if Judd hadn't gotten himself messed up with those thugs and that whole debacle. But that would be dreaming on my part, wouldn't it?"

"Well, Dad, not to sympathize with him, but he was under major stress. He'd screwed Holton as well, and his crew, and he was trying to bluff them, but it didn't work. He was still in their crosshairs. Too bad my mother hadn't been around then. Knowing her, she could've put her head to this whole mess. And what about her escapade? Today, someone would have talked to us. To tell us she loved us. To try to figure out what happened. But no. The police just figured she'd run off—which in the end was the real answer."

"I was convinced she'd died," Colin said. "The whole story was so unthinkable. I didn't know what to say." He seemed to shrink into his chair. "So, I kept up with our usual father and daughter activities and let it ride."

"Let it ride? You let it ride? What could you be thinking?"

"I know. It was a bad plan. It never resolved things." He looked at his daughter as if to gauge her reaction. "I wanted to bolt from it. Irresponsible—like your mother, right?" He ran a hand over his forehead. "I was in the dark as much as the rest of you. Furious and frightened at the same time. It's going to be a while before I can trust MT again. I suppose you've noticed she's avoiding me?"

Sage was silent. He pressed on.

"No more twosome trips for groceries in my immediate future, I fear. She'll drag her car out of the garage—provided she doesn't get mugged again—and take off on her own. Which, of course, isn't a good idea."

"I'll get her one of those safety things you wear around your neck. And I'm sure Qadri or my mother will be happy to go along. Mom's got a lot to learn about this part of the country. It's changed over the years."

"Good grief, this whole mess is such a scramble I can't keep track of anything. I need a straitjacket and a good bottle of zin to reset my brain. Good wine always helps."

"Not a bad idea. Anyhow, don't you see?" Sage went on. "This whole mess is the result of deception. We're all guilty. I was a kid who doted on her dad. I was blind to the whole thing—but I guess that's a kind of guilt itself. But hey, we did have fun, didn't we? You kept me occupied with maps and colored pins. And there were those hidden messages."

Colin smiled and nodded.

"My decorated cigar box from second grade was a crafty form of communication," Sage said "How many kids can boast about that special part of childhood? Artists are supposed to be in their own world—well, you have been—but you were still there for me."

"Was I? Thanks, but I'm not so sure."

"Have you been listening? So what if you were an unusual father. You were there for *me*. Thank God we found you—and yeah, I have to say the help from Alex was a big part."

"What's up with him now?"

"Haven't heard. I know he was heading back to the Middle East. This time it was some kind of personal mission. Felt he had unfinished business. Not sure how that's going to work, given his mental state. At least he's made a decision to fix things for himself. I hope we learn how it turns out."

"That's the thing," Colin mused. "I've always lived in the moment. You know—instant gratification. I'm not sure I have the guts to fix the past. But that's not saying I somehow learned my lesson from this mess. It's just that I pretty much see it now for what it is. I'm still putting together the big picture. I don't really know how to deal with it all. Does that count?"

"Sure. It's like me. I hate to mess with your gusto, but I think it's a lifelong project. Part of the key is watching how other people do it." Sage reached for her father's hand. "Meanwhile, how about we make a father-daughter effort to update our old studio games?"

Colin breathed a long sigh. "If only I could go back," he said, "I must be civilization's oldest late bloomer."

"No, Dad. I hate to tell you this, but you're not going to change. Not really. You just had a chance to see things from a different angle."

He laughed. "Huh. Right… from inside a box."

"I don't think I can tell if you're really different," Sage smiled.

"Maybe not different my dear daughter, but definitely wiser."

"I think you've just learned to be a sharper observer while you drift along. It's just that now you have a canoe that's not so leaky."

* * *

171

It was the first winter storm of the season. Light from the trail cams revealed three figures bucking the snow. The tallest walked in the middle, fighting gusts while guiding two shorter figures, all with their arms linked. Together, they fought the driving snow, sometimes stumbling, then regaining their footing to press ahead toward Colin's studio.

"Good grief, look at that," Sage said and beckoned to her father. "Who are they? I can't see through that blast of snow."

"Don't tell me I've got customers on a night like this." He chuckled. "Not sure I want to open this studio door and let all that inside. Glad we agreed to put a fridge and that old stove out here."

"It's not quite a blizzard—just a major snow dump along with strong wind," Sage said. Although the light from the house didn't reach the studio, she recognized Alex's silhouette. "Oh, my God, look who's here!" she shouted. "It's Alex, and if I'm right, he's bringing the best surprise I've ever seen!"

Qadri ran to the window. When he saw the three people stomping through the snow, he let out a scream of joy.

Colin chuckled. "Not sure I want to open the door and let all that inside."

MT smiled. "I'm glad you invited me for dinner. I don't plan on going anywhere until April."

"Hey, that kid is going to fly through the window," Colin said. "What the hell is out there?"

"A big surprise, for sure," Sage grinned. "He had a great time with us over the holidays, but this is a thousand times better."

"I think this is the best Christmas gift a kid ever had," Colin said as he cracked the door open. Qadri screamed and dashed toward his parents. His father held out his hands, and the boy flew into his arms.

"Everyone, this is Aalem," Alex said, and the man held his hand out to Colin. "And Najia, Qadri's mother."

Najia wiped her tears and whispered her thanks.

Sage watched her father step forward with both arms outstretched. "We welcome you, and we will help you in your new home."

Aalem smiled and grasped Colin's hands.

"Please sit, and we will make tea," Colin said. He turned to Alex. "Have they had food?"

Both parents nodded while Qadri attempted to squeeze between them on the sofa. Colin stood near the fireplace and watched the family's endless joy.

"You okay now, buddy?" Alex smiled.

The boy nodded and turned toward his father's chest. "It will be good," Aalem said. "We are now together." He stroked his son's head. "We are safe. And see? We have new friends."

Quadri lowered his head, and Sage watched him wipe his cheek with the back of his hand.

Alex spoke slowly. "Your family has come many miles, and everything's new, isn't it?" Qadri nodded back. "I remember when I came to your country, and everything was new for me. It takes a while to feel like you belong. And your father says you have a sister. She's on her way now with your grandma. We'll all be so happy when they come. You'll have lots to show them."

Qadri smiled slowly and spoke in a voice muffled by his father's chest. "He's bilingual—often at the same time," Alex smiled.

* * *

As if on duty, Colin woke at dawn. "I bet we can stomp a path up to the house," he said. "And then how about one of my special woodland breakfasts? The kind I like to make for the favorite people in my life." He gazed down at Qadri. "Do you want to break a path for us?"

The boy's face glowed as he looked up to his father. "That is okay? I'm hungry!"

Aalem nodded. "Go ahead, I am behind you." Qadri's mother Najia walked closely after them, wearing the boots given to her when she arrived in Minnesota.

"Want me to squeeze OJ?" Sage pulled her boots from behind the sofa.

They tromped out the door into a wonderland of snow-laden pine and rocks masquerading as gigantic marshmallows. Last in line, MT pulled a sweeping woolen cape around her shoulders. The chimes gave a faint jingle as she lovingly took them from their place on the hook. "Come along, then, Wats," she whispered as she headed for the door. "Our work isn't done."

AFTERWORD

Minnesota's Arrowhead Region comprises 10,635 square miles of land over Carlton, Cook, Lake, and St. Louis counties. The rugged beauty of the area is surrounded by boreal forest and is home to Voyageurs National Park. Dotted with thousands of lakes, the Boundary Waters Canoe Area Wilderness (BWCA) and the Superior Hiking Trail are located in the Superior National Forest.

The Arrowhead also offers Minnesota's only mountain range, the Sawtooth Mountains. The region is a prized vacation destination for Minnesota residents as well as visitors from across the US and abroad. The location is part of three watersheds: the Lake Superior Basin, the Mississippi River Basin, and the Hudson Bay (Rainy River) Basin. North of Hibbing, Minnesota, a rare geological feature allows water to flow in any one of three ways. The only other location where this phenomenon occurs in North America is at Glacier National Park in Montana.

ABOUT THE AUTHOR

Carol Rincker has a background in geology and interests in anthropology, biology, environmental studies, and science journalism. She is the author of the children's book *Science in Ancient Mesopotamia* and has edited a range of academic books and research papers. When not at her computer, she breaks away to explore Duluth and the Arrowhead country along the North Shore of Lake Superior.